WAKEFIELD CRIME CLASSICS

VANISHING POINT

———

Pat Flower was born in Kent in 1928 and came to Australia when she was fourteen. She committed suicide in 1978.

She lived mainly in Sydney, and won wide international acclaim for her fiction and her writing for radio, television and theatre.

Most of her many mystery novels were first published in London in the Collins Crime Club series and translated across Europe. Later ones were also published in the United States.

'Pat Flower is adept at depicting ordinary people who are slightly skewed – usually to the point where they commit murder. She also tells a riveting tale.'

Melbourne *Age*

'A remarkable study of a possessive and unbalanced woman, with a colourful background of the north of Australia.'

Sydney Morning Herald

wer stands out as exceptional.'

London *Sunday Times*

PAT FLOWER

WAKEFIELD
CRIME
CLASSICS

...ies editors Michael J. Tolley and Peter Moss

Wakefield Press
Box 2266
Kent Town
South Australia 5071

First published by William Collins Limited, London, 1975
Published in Wakefield Crime Classics February 1993

Edited by Jane Arms
Designed by Design Bite, Melbourne
Printed and bound by Hyde Park Press, Adelaide

Cataloguing-in-publication data
Flower, Pat
Vanishing point
ISBN 1 86254 292 9.
I. Title. (Series: Wakefield Crime Classics; no.8).
A823.2

ISSN for Wakefield Crime Classics series 1039-4451

———

Part one

———

CHAPTER I

The tent was orange and claustrophobic. Geraldine lay inside
it on her stretcher and wished Noel were with her, making
love. He was right to say there was not enough room for comfort. But Geraldine remembered their first wild love when
room and comfort went out the window. Then he'd wanted
her so much it was to hell with room and comfort, and if
they'd got into these circumstances then it would have been
to hell with the smell of insect repellent and whether the others would hear. 'Six times a day before and after meals,' he
said, 'that's not counting nights.' With his slow sexy smile.
Sex was their private joy and consummation, not a vulgarity
for parties. Noel had gone downhill in a lot of ways. And
Geraldine loved him too much to overlook his faults. It was
wrong to smile at his puns. The damage was to both of them
and Noel must be made to realise. Ten years was too long a
time and here was the opportunity to pull him up short. This
trip would be the turning-point. Elation flooded through her.
If this were obsession, then it was delicious, and it was worthy
too. And Geraldine smiled at the thought of love regenerated
on something as poisonous as a long trek in tents. Bleakly
aware that then, ten years ago, these circumstances would
have been unthinkable.

She looked through the little net window in the slanting
orange canvas and tried to remember whether punning had
been part of the whole of him she'd loved from their first

meeting. Wasn't she too observant of the unpleasant traits people have? She couldn't have been so deaf even in love. So Noel had bitten it back for her sake, sweet darling Noel. She hadn't been deaf to his first spoonerism, had she? Let's hang on to the first glossy row, he'd said on their honeymoon in New Caledonia. And then had gone off for the day without her, without telling her, only the third day. She could smile now at the hurt of then.

Was Noel asleep? All their tents were orange, all five of them. The whisky would put him to sleep. He was drinking whisky on the trip because it went further than wine, his usual tipple. There was a case of whisky in Don's Land-Rover and when it ran out they'd get another. They imagined Cape York Peninsula rife with liquor supplies. The silly assumptions people made. Geraldine was thankful she was blessed with a reasoning mind. She'd be glad when they ran out of whisky. Noel would too in the long run, when their private stocktaking started. It was ridiculous to set out on an expedition of this kind, over vast distances with campfires and tents, and bring bad habits with you. Noel's punning too. Geraldine would have thought the changing landscape, the new experience, the very bigness of the sky that looked so much smaller in Sydney, would jolt Noel out of it. Cape York Puninsula, he called it. Now and again he said with his smile, 'Where's the point?' and squeezed Geraldine's arm or touched her breast. Dear silly Noel. Last night in the dying fire she thought he'd touched Julie. She hated Noel to touch anyone else.

Yesterday evening – no, afternoon, because it was winter and darker earlier, their first day out and just north of the Hawkesbury. Don had wanted an early start, but it was after lunch before they got away: Noel's phone calls, his friends bon-voyaging. Tonight they were at Port Macquarie, but days didn't matter, time didn't count, or places. Slow travel or fast was immaterial, the important thing was making Noel see. North of the Hawkesbury yesterday there were orange orchards, uniform rows of round trees shining dark green and hung with orange baubles. Wayside stalls with big net bags of oranges for sale. And pumpkins. A round white stall itself like a pale squash laden with small blue-green pumpkins and bags of oranges hanging. Apples, grapefruit, onions, potatoes. Beautiful wooded valleys. Glints of water, sheets of water, pale blue glass with patches of pink. Big pink clouds scudding fast. Sunset a misty spray of flame over water and trees and hills and islands. It seemed to Geraldine the most romantic place in the world. Cabbage tree palms, crisp air, big stately gums, their thick mauve-grey trunks streaked in red. Geraldine with a full heart because Noel felt the same, no one could be immune, snuggling up to him, knowing they'd recapture the early bliss, kissing his neck.

'Darling, look,' she'd said, 'you can spare a quick glance, the clouds up there, those spectacular rents.'

And Noel had said, 'It's those thieving landlords again,' and hugged her close for a moment, driving with one hand, laughing. He thought his pun especially funny because Geraldine was a landlord. Often he ribbed her about bleeding the poor.

The others were Don, Julie and Bernard, all three in one Land-Rover. Don and Bernard shared the driving and the one who wasn't took turns with Julie between the front seat and a seat they had in the back. Both Rovers were packed to the rafters with all kinds of gear, clothing and food supplies. Don was resolute about camping: boots and all, no motels and cafés, no softening of tough conditions, do the thing properly. That didn't matter either. Geraldine would put up with any privations because of the end in view. She could smile at the picture of herself, so fastidious and orderly, on a trip like this where everything got to be slapdash no matter how one tried. The last thing she'd have chosen. Europe, perhaps, or New Caledonia again, or just a cruise round the islands. But she'd make it work in the same way. Turn it into an adventure in which they'd regain their private joy. She knew what strings to pull. Put it squarely to Noel that they were drifting apart for no real reason, then subtly suggest why: his time filled with worthless people calling themselves his friends. Let Noel realise for himself how they used him up to the detriment of his wonderful relationship with Geraldine. No need to mention money or her house, Noel would see well enough. It would work, it must. A word from her, then together assess the way their life was shaping. The next few weeks would see a sorting out and a shedding and in time be a cherished memory. People got bogged down, lost sight of the long view. The only thing was to leave the clutter behind. Then spatial grandeur, with a nudge or two from Geraldine, would restore Noel's perspective.

Hardship in tents. Geraldine smiled, remembering Dennis's disbelief when he heard she was going on safari too. Even in the dark the canvas looked orange. The nice fishy ocean smell of Port Macquarie came in the little net square. Noel away from Dennis, all to herself. Together analyse his frailties, start the cure. So far she'd been silent; it was heaven enough to have Noel beside her, to know every moment where he was. It was only the second day, there were weeks ahead.

All the same they should have made love last night, Hawkesbury River night, their first night out, the first away alone. Geraldine had it planned when she drew his attention to the clouds, and with a moment's thought she'd never have said spectacular rents. A moment's sanity and she'd have sensed Noel's poisoned pun. But love such as hers for Noel should have no need to choose words. Noel's punning was to blame. He must see how childish it was, even destructive. Geraldine had an idea that after Brisbane she could better reason with him. She had a feeling about Brisbane, that it was a point they must pass before she could guide Noel back. Noel took her love for granted like an everyday thing, something he was sure of like a big fast car and his favourite marmalade for breakfast. His complacency needed a puncture. He had to know how much she loved him: so *much* she could eat him all up.

For Don, Bernard and Julie this was a holiday, a break from responsibilities. They were less than nothing to Geraldine; strangers, chance co-travellers. Maybe they'd fossick around for gemstones, Julie said, and Don had heard of a few caves with Aboriginal paintings. But it was to be relaxed, easy, no deadlines. Only Geraldine had a deadline. They were good-natured enough but slouches, untidy and dirty. When Geraldine remarked on this to Noel he said, 'Who cares, angel?' 'I don't, darling,' Geraldine said, 'I only care about you.'

Angel and Goddess were Noel's pet names for Geraldine because of her build, because he said she was the spitting image of those massive big-breasted dames in old paintings and sculptures. He still delighted in her air of appeal, her manner of total dependence; it tickled him because she was tall and strong, with big firm breasts, strong hands and unfailing health. She remembered a party once and lifting a laden tray one-handed. Someone had remarked on her strength, and Noel had said, had told the whole roomful of people, 'Don't be fooled, inside it's a scared little rabbit – isn't it angel?' Noel laughing and all their eyes on her, on the fiction of the visible, settling on her breasts. And then someone had said, 'Rot, Gerry's an Amazon,' and Geraldine had frozen behind her big calm social smile, as much at Amazon as at Gerry. Noel couldn't comprehend how real the dependence was, that without him Geraldine's life would fall apart. It was a matter of survival, and the only reason she was here in this stifling tent of poisonous orange, on this ill-organised trip. With strangers, illegally pitched in a caravan park.

Geraldine turned over on the creaking stretcher. She was leaving behind all the little resentments, they were a cloud fast vanishing from clear skies.

Noel had met Don in the unreliable atmosphere of Noel's Den. It was one night in the lax, vinuous aftermath when most other diners had drifted off. It was also one of the rare times Geraldine was there. Noel was dog-tired. Sick of the daily smell and sight of food, Geraldine thought, and perhaps regretting he'd ever plunged into the eatery with Dennis. Geraldine had been against the silly Noel's Den venture from the start, and if Noel had taken her advice he'd still be in his former job, respectable and steady. And far more often at home. Then he'd never have met Don, and Cape York Peninsula would never have entered his head. As it was, he'd listened to Don's outline of the expedition catching only bits here and there in the general clatter and muddle. All the same he jumped at Don's offer instantly, clutching at a stranger's straw. Geraldine had offered straws. Yet this crazy traipse to the Cape caught his fancy. Just like that, not a moment's thought. A bit drunk, of course, poor darling.

Geraldine guessed Don was after some generous fool who wouldn't question expenses. Pressed close beside Noel, her hand tucked under his arm, with a tolerant smile she'd suggested sleeping on it. But Noel was adamant: just what he needed, a great draught of fresh air and freedom. Geraldine's last hope, that Dennis would raise objections, fell flat. Dennis thought it a great idea; his pal Nick, who was the waiter, would stand in for Noel during Noel's absence. Dennis was always so accommodating. Noel thought Geraldine was joking when she said she'd go too. Frowning, he said she'd hate it, and dragged in deadly snakes and armies of bull ants to enforce his argument. Then all at once he was enthusiastic. Perhaps hoping he'd be able to say, I told you so.

Geraldine got up. She threw the towelling robe over her naked body, untied the tent's flap and went outside. Everything was sleeping: caravans, big square family tents of bright green or dirty white, dogs, children, transistors; and their own small pointy orange tents that looked an alien cluster among the domestic suburbanism of caravanners. Well, they were alien, they weren't supposed to camp in a caravan park. It was Don's burly charm had done the trick, and maybe a few dollars.

The sky was awake, the great sky clear and lovely. The sea, too, surf pounding. There was no wind, and the walk beyond the park's confines cleared her head, the mood of elation returned to sustain her. Little things didn't matter, didn't last. Darling Noel. She longed to go into his tent, nearest to hers. But the place was wrong, it wasn't yet time, not remote enough, still too many people. After Brisbane.

Geraldine went back to bed, smiling. She might not sleep with her random thoughts, but they were benign now, the worries off her chest. She'd lie at peace, make no complaint tomorrow.

'Spaghetti's up, goddess.' Daylight suddenly and Noel's grin through the flap. 'Lovely hot spaghetti out of tins so better hurry and grab some. Julie's promised a damper for tonight.'

Her smile too late, he'd gone, no kiss. The tiniest sinking feeling. But that was silly; Noel would be helping with breakfast, he'd seemed in the middle of something.

It was hot in the tent. She didn't hurry. She hated tinned spaghetti. She'd hate Julie's damper – no, that was wrong, anybody's damper, all dampers: flour and water kneaded with dirty fingers and baked in a hole burrowed under hot ashes. But she'd eat it, reject nothing, no little thing that Noel might hold against her.

Geraldine dropped the towel on her stretcher and rolled deodorant over her washed armpits. Lovely water in nearby motels ran hot and cold but, no matter, if Noel could adapt to the exiguity of two plastic drums then so could she.

'Hey, Gerry, it's stone cold.' That was Don. Geraldine went on brushing her hair but got her nice smile ready. Then went outside with it, conscious of looking neat and clean. Noel couldn't miss the contrast between herself and the others, especially Julie.

'Well, look who's here, Madam Fashion-Plate,' Don said.

'I'll just hot up the spaghetti,' Julie said in her friendly voice and her stringy long dark hair hanging over the pink mess.

'Just coffee,' Geraldine smiled, 'I'll get it.'

'Shoving on to Murwillumbah today,' Don said.

'Lovely,' Geraldine said.

Bernard was picking his nose.

'Come on, then, let's up and at it,' Don said.

Geraldine stood drinking the black instant coffee and watched the vanishing trick: pots and pans and provisions stacked in their cartons, strewn oddments collected, rubbish hauled off to litter bins, the tents come down.

'Your stuff ready, angel?' Noel squeezed her waist.

'Of course, darling.'

She watched Noel working with the others. Because Noel did her share, the others took her exemption for granted. It was cold after all, but sunny. Don exchanged matey words with some of the caravanners. It was early, not quite seven. The sun came through a thin mist. Inland where it was higher there'd be frost.

Julie was about thirty-seven, Geraldine thought; untidy, laughed a lot, a kind manner, the stringy hair and a genial, weatherbeaten face, Geraldine had no idea of Julie's relationship to either man, or both. It was of no interest to her. Don was burly and coarse, not as tall as Noel but much broader, with massive shoulders. He could change a tyre easy as winking. Noel said he was an interstate haulier. Bernard was tall, thin and dark and did something in a government office; he was a bad colour and said little, just an occasional cliché. Geraldine saw how adaptable Noel was, able to talk with them and laugh at their jokes. She would too, it wasn't for long.

It was a flat watery district, mouth of the Hastings River. Lots of holiday-makers, fresh fish daily, some early history and a few relics.

Dear Noel. Geraldine watched him make neat tight bundles of her night in the orange tent. A thrill ran up into her throat. Noel was thirty-four, four years older than Geraldine but such a baby: likeable and liking everybody, gregarious, easygoing, too ready to take quick risks. Tall, dark, not handsome but so good-looking. The thrill was the same one, unchanged from the time she first met him, met his tall dark irresistible presence with the slow smile so sexy it encompassed the whole act of copulation. A man she couldn't ignore, couldn't resist, had to have. Still had to have, for always. Mercurial, she'd thought him then. Now she knew he was elusive, a shade dishonest in dodging unpleasantness. But still irresistible.

Noel was married before. It had all blown up in a year. Just one of those things he said. Noel made light of everything, even his poisonous former wife. He was thrilled about Geraldine's money. He wooed them both, her money too. He said her light hazel eyes were divine; her short thick dark-blonde hair, big breasts, wide mouth: all divine. Her large face was in proportion, he said; he said it was well boned. Her healthiness was divine, and her riches just as divine as the rest of her. She was a goddess, an angel. Darling silly Noel. Her money wasn't riches, but it was safe and sure.

On the way out of town they filled up with petrol. Murwillumbah was about 450 kilometres, quite a longish drive and a lot would depend on traffic. These things didn't matter to Geraldine. Only Noel mattered, and once they were on their way she could look at him, so close she could touch him at any time, all the time if she chose, and know something would come of this odd adventure his whim had got them into. Stay calm as always. If Noel were evasive, hang on, reason with him. Indulgent as always but firm. He'd been drifting, he mustn't drift out of her reach.

On an impulse she jerked towards him, both hands squeezing his arm. 'I do love you, darling – darling Noel, I love you so terribly much.'

'That's nice, goddess.' Noel was frowning at the road, negotiating a curve among the heavy traffic.

Geraldine felt choked with her love for him.

———

CHAPTER 2

When Geraldine was eleven her father Gerald Smith, aged forty-three, had an affair with a tall thin woman in pink who rode a motor-scooter. After weeks of snooping, Mrs Smith was rewarded one night by a shocking sight among dunes at the back of a beach. Geraldine hated him for it, she'd heard a lot from her mother about dirty old men. Pink and motor-scooters went on to her permanent blacklist. Mother had rightly given him hell and, a year later, after his lonely ugly death from lung cancer, Mother said through her tears that it was a judgement. That was in 1957 when Geraldine was twelve.

Mr Smith did well during World War 2. As a Commonwealth Public Servant, young and ambitious but with a lucky vision defect that kept him from active service, he got in on some kind of supply racket. After all, Mother told Geraldine when the loot came into her hands after his death, the troops and war workers had to be fed, hadn't they? The racket was going on anyway, so where was the point in standing off and losing out? Conscience may have caused Mr Smith's decline to drink, infidelity and lung cancer, but Mother was concerned only for own and her daughter's needs. Once all the tedious bother of death was over, Mrs Smith invested in two blocks of flats, side by side in liverish brick in a safely distant northern suburb. Forty flats in all. Mother's good business sense, and an estate agent in the crowd she played bridge with, told her that property values would appreciate. Rents too. But pneumonia snatched her from luxury only two years later, and Geraldine, with the same reliable agent to handle things, was comfortably off for life. Mr Grant let Geraldine know how well he protected her from the slings and arrows of tenants, often beyond his precise function. In a smooth voice, he said there was no reason for her to be subjected to grovelling pleas or threats to do with bloodsucking. Geraldine was grateful. She hated that kind of thing, wanted no part of the seamy side.

It was a bit hypocritical of Noel to keep up the landlord jibe. Her income was a very nice backstop, wasn't it?

Geraldine met Noel Blaine through Andrew Lee, a quiet, well-spoken carpenter who'd done her a built-in wardrobe with louvered doors. Andrew was a big man with lank brown hair and dull brown eyes, fairly well educated, well read, musical and not in the least pushy. Geraldine accepted his trade because of these other refinements. Sometimes Andrew tried his hand at a small bit of sculpture, with apologies and self-deprecation. Poor Andrew, so plainly in love with her. He phoned one day to see if she'd make a foursome at a symphony concert. The other two were Gail Wallace, the cow-like girl Andrew lived with, and Noel. The mutual chemistry had been instantaneous.

Geraldine looked sideways at Noel. How well he drove, only the frown, but that was concentration. They were crossing a bridge, the Macleay River at Kempsey. The air rushing in at the sides was cool still despite the sun. And Noel's dear head so close. It made her swoony with rapture. The ocean smell and the beautiful country. Geraldine didn't see the fibro shacks and the garish service stations, only the way clear ahead, pristine and beckoning. Over the sea from the northeast a sort of damp gloomy shroud crept closer, but all she saw was the sunshine flooding all over them because they were alone, just with each other, going forward together, the life they'd left in Sydney petty beyond belief. Lunch would be soon, but such small infringements on her private world of Noel had to be faced with a smile. The others just a brief trial to be got through. Geraldine watched Noel with a little smile that persisted. Noel, aware of it, threw a grin in return and squeezed her jeaned right thigh. But his frown stayed.

It was the same frown he'd worn a lot lately, as though its cause had come with him on the trip. Some worry over Noel's Den perhaps, or Dennis himself. Geraldine didn't like Dennis, she didn't like Noel's friends. Noel let them take advantage of him, he was too easily persuaded, enthusiastic too soon. This trip, for instance. Not a really resolute face. Being nice to Noel's friends was a taxing job for Geraldine, it was treading a tightrope between repression and over-indulgence. Dear irresponsible Noel hadn't a clue about the strain on Geraldine.

Noel said on their wedding day, just over ten years ago, with a big hug, 'So Geraldine Smith married Noel Blaine and they lived happily ever after.' And they would, they must. Geraldine clung to the mood of uplift that might so easily slip, at the same time sure that every kilometre further away anchored it more firmly. She glanced at him again, the sideways look, at his hair that had got too long. It didn't suit him so long, it looked wrong, somehow not her Noel. Perhaps the frown was only the Land-Rover getting on his nerves; Noel was a fast driver and might be irritated by the need to temper his speed to the vehicle. Geraldine liked the slowness, the steady and manageable progression that seemed to reinforce her certainty of victory. Besides, Don was in front and Don set the pace.

Following Don now, Noel pulled in at a service station diner. Geraldine went to the Ladies' with tissues, soap and towel. By the time she got inside the café Noel was already opposite Julie at one of the hard plastic tables. They were laughing together, Noel leaning forward, come alive. Don was outside with his bonnet open and a mechanic. Bernard was at another table reading the menu with moving lips. The chair beside Noel was empty. Geraldine slid into it and snuggled against him. She smiled at Julie. 'Tired?' she asked.

Julie laughed no.

'You've done this before, have you, this sort of thing?'

'Only weekends, not like this,' Julie said.

'You're pretty good at it, isn't she, Noel?'

Julie smiled and Noel put his arm round Geraldine and touched her in a very private caress.

'We're in public,' Geraldine breathed.

'Just keeping abreast, angel.'

Pun or not she was faint with wanting him. She hated Julie's sly grin. But because Noel liked her friendliness to Julie she said, 'I can't wait for that damper.'

Julie laughed. 'Better keep your fingers crossed.'

Geraldine raked over her mind for another trivial pleasantry but found none. Noel and Julie went on with their easy jokes. But Geraldine was pressed against him and wasn't that all that mattered?

Don came in. 'Gonna rain like stink.' He sat with Bernard.

Noel was laughing as he hadn't laughed since breakfast. Geraldine's toasted ham sandwich tasted of petrol, the coffee too. Then there was the stench of Noel's and Julie's sausages and eggs. Geraldine turned her head away and got a side view of Don's paunch, cut into two bulges by the top of his shorts. His pink shirt hung loose, revealing a purple singlet.

It would soon be over.

After lunch Don lingered with the mechanic who'd fixed whatever it was. One of his interminable chats about engines. Bernard followed the talk closely, picking his teeth with a fingernail. Geraldine was already in their Land-Rover, waiting. She wouldn't look round for him, it was Julie who wouldn't let him go. Julie was a great old chatterer. Geraldine would see the bad weather now, they were nearly into it.

It started around Nambucca Heads. It was almost as dark as night. Don't think of portents, they're mostly empty imaginings. There seemed a smell of whisky, but Noel had promised never till sundown. She stole a look at him. Noel looked grim and tired. The weather change on top of his lunch, he'd had too big a lunch. But she'd say nothing, just sit here quietly beside him being happy.

The weather beat against Noel's side. Through Geraldine's window the land looked pleased with the rain, and she caught a parrot's primary colours flashing into a tree.

'You ate too much, darling.'

Noel grunted.

'Just eggs was enough.'

'Oh, Christ!'

Geraldine smiled and stroked his arm. 'It's not a reproach, just something you should know.'

'I *do* know, you keep on telling me.'

Geraldine said nothing. She wouldn't be upset by Noel's childishness. She loved him too much, the real Noel beneath the vulgar veneer. He might be regretting the trip, he often rued his impulses. That meant he'd appreciate their accounting even more, and every steady kilometre brought it closer. Perhaps his frown was a matter of the wrong food.

They passed Coffs Harbour where it was all bananas, hills and humidity, and parrots squawking joyously in the rain. The rain was falling sheets now, and it was still raining at Grafton. The highway skirted the town and crossed the Clarence River.

Under the dashboard a map stuck out from Noel's mess in the rack there. Geraldine opened it, careful to keep it out of his way. Still a fair distance to Murwillumbah. Geraldine hoped the rain wouldn't slow them down and hoped they'd all have the sense to use a motel. She folded the map in its creases and put it back. With the sides shut for the rain Noel seemed somehow closer, the snug dry interior their haven against the world and its wetness and follies. Noel hadn't asked how much further. He was so intent on the slippery road and perhaps indigestion. Ever since Noel's Den started, breakfast was Noel's only meal Geraldine could oversee. So much had fallen off since Noel's Den. It all began with meeting Dennis, and he met Dennis because of added responsibility in his former job and a switch in advertising. It wasn't the fault of the extra responsibility, or really of the new agency, it was because Noel was an easy mark for people like Dennis. Geraldine made a point of not remembering Dennis's surname. Noel kept on goodnaturedly telling her. Lemon, perhaps. Or was it Lemming? Wasn't that a kind of rat? She didn't want to remember, didn't care, shut her ears. It might be Snake, the one in the grass. She forgot to jot down Dennis's phone messages when Noel was out. Dennis saw Noel most of each day, often till late at night; he had plenty of Noel's time to chatter in.

Geraldine was glad when they stopped somewhere for cups of tea and pees. It brought her back to here, miles from Noel's Den. Nobody was hungry. Geraldine was but said nothing. Things that would ordinarily depress her flew by unnoticed, even the pink of Don's shirt. The serene mood kept its hold.

Real darkness set in on top of the rain's gloom. It was easy to lose count of time with the vehicle's motion, in the rain, seeing nothing, stuck in a seat with Noel's smoke making the headache she got at Noel's parties. It brought back Clyde's cigar.

Clyde Nixon was a financial and legal wizard, they said, reputed to know all the lurks. He'd advised Noel and Dennis at the start of Noel's Den. He was in the same advertising agency, on the administrative side, where Noel had met Dennis. Heavy drinker, loud laugh, hair the colour of dirty straw, purple face, cigar, high blood pressure, portly. The friendly squeeze and hearty backslap type, someone to be dodged at all times. Talked a lot about fiscal policies, world trends, overseas money, commercial tussles and liquidity, yet somehow always with dirty sex threaded through. A most dreadful bore, a filthy mind. Always at Noel's parties. Asked or not, he seemed to smell them out. A hanger-on.

Noel had too many: Claire Sayers, Elaine Thorpe, the Hudsons, the Monros, he called them all his friends: a poisonous bunch taking up all his time. Noel was worth something better; he was worth all her effort. Even Andrew and Gail were Noel's friends now, not hers.

One felt so dirty travelling. She'd endure that too. The cramped conditions, the overflowing anxiety and ashtray.

Noel was open about the eatery gamble and discussed every aspect frankly with Geraldine. Her money was a moral back-up, he said, but only that, because they'd gone into it thoroughly and with Clyde's advice they couldn't fail. 'It'll be a winner, goddess, we wouldn't be such fools.' This was before he'd resigned from his job so Geraldine could have her say. Geraldine said a lot. Every argument she could think of. Noel countered them all.

Noel was making steady progress in the same job he had when Geraldine first met him. He was assistant advertising manager. It was the Australian headquarters of a giant over-seas packaged foods firm with tentacles in other industries. A safe job with long-range prospects. To throw it up for a crackpot suburban eating house was insane, a criminal gamble, even if it was on a strategic corner. If the corner were so strategic why was the old shop empty? Clyde, of course, had an explanation for that, some involved lie about changes in the pattern of community living, a once-rented property now for sale and supermarkets replacing smaller shops. Geraldine sought an ally in Mr Grant who handled her flats, but all she got was confirmation of Clyde's view, with migrants somehow thrown in for good measure. It was especially galling that if Noel's firm hadn't switched advertising agencies, he wouldn't have met Dennis and Clyde in the new one. He'd still be climbing steadily in packaged foods and keeping reasonable hours. At home with her in between times.

Dennis was a visualizer. Noel said he was staunch as a rock, but Geraldine had a different opinion, distrusting artists on principle. It was only because Andrew Lee was genuinely a carpenter that she would tolerate his sculptural flights, and Andrew himself was bashful about what he called his outlet. Dennis wasn't like that. Dennis was willowy, with a false untrustworthy smile, and Geraldine guessed his engagement to Claire Sayers was a useful blind. And when later on, near opening day, in a late light bibulous session at Geraldine's house, they hit on the name Noel's Den, thinking it brilliant, Geraldine flinched at the inference. But continued to smile because Dennis was always watching for her smile to slip. Dennis was worse than Clyde because he was sly.

They wanted to be their own bosses. It seemed a paltry motivation. Clyde's business acumen made it a walkover, Noel said, because dear old Clyde sailed through the property finance deal and all the rest of it like a dream. Noel told Geraldine every move, and with every move she felt more alone and deserted. Left out of Noel's life all the long days, and probably evenings too. She felt her hold over Noel slip. Premonition told her the move was a bad one, no matter what the experts said. Their testimony took no account of Geraldine's personal life with Noel.

She thought Dennis was taking the hold she was losing. She suspected Dennis, but of what she wasn't sure. Wasn't it enough that Dennis had upset their life, was stealing Noel from her? Dennis's manner towards Geraldine was ambivalent, not friendly but not unfriendly, not male and not quite female, never serious but never entirely joking.

It was a single-storey place with plenty of back room and a big yard in a rundown suburb being rediscovered and not terribly far as the crow flies. Geraldine said Noel wasn't a crow and was just as subject to red lights and traffic jams as the next man. It wasn't too big inside; just nice, Noel said. They'd have a *plat du jour* with wine by the glass and real coffee. Dennis designed it inside and out including shrubs in pots and a red-lit 'Noel's Den' at the entrance. Noel's contacts in the food world came in useful, and dear old Clyde handled the liquor licence. Noel had the brilliant economising idea of using today's leftovers in tomorrow's dish. They thought all their hackneyed old notions brilliant. They were like silly children, silly, cruel children.

It was how the rot started. Noel's previous railing against life was like anyone's, as standard as the common cold. This was going too far. It thumbed a nose at the rules of established order, but worse, it thumbed a nose at Geraldine. Just about then Noel had his first insight into one of Geraldine's bouts of depression. It lasted weeks, she couldn't lift it. Noel had the worry of it during the start of Noel's Den. Geraldine was dreadfully sorry and told Noel she really was trying to pull out of it, trying to find something positive in what he was doing. If only she cared what people ate or whether they ate or not, or cared what happened to that slippery Dennis Something Noel found so admirable.

It was when she saw it was going ahead anyway that Geraldine changed tactics. Often she dropped in there, expressing admiration and encouragement. She raked through all her cookbooks, invented dishes and made special trips to Noel's Den to tell them short cuts. It just fed her jealousy. One day she overheard Dennis say, 'Gerry's wonderful, isn't she?' and then Noel's laughing reply, 'Call her Gerry she'll kill you,' and after a thoughtful moment Dennis's quiet voice, 'I don't think so.' Dennis knew how she watched them; she knew he watched her too, that he was aware of every move she made, any reaction. Then in a flash she realised what was troubling Dennis: the poor thing was in love with her. Of course, as always. Poor Dennis with his brave enigmatic smile, he must know that for Geraldine there was only Noel.

But it made no difference to the agony she endured. Most of all she hated the touching. Even when Noel brushed past somebody Geraldine saw the contact of naked flesh, of arms, hips, buttocks with all the erotic responses each must feel. By going to Noel's Den she could torment herself. In his other job Noel had been cut off from her: not seeing was not knowing. Now there were customers, even Nick the waiter, a handsome young Greek introduced by Dennis. Pretty girl customers, so young, too free and easy, too lithe. And Dennis. She saw how Noel and Dennis touched each other in the busy rush, felt a rush of blood to her head, then the sick feeling, the dark despairing, the sinking, the nadir. But if Noel waved to her over intervening people they vanished; or he'd kiss her hair in passing, or whisper a rushed endearment into her ear. Then at once she'd be whisked up high again to the realm where no worry intruded. Superior to them all because Noel saw through them too. So superior she could leave Noel's Den and go back home.

But there, alone, the imaginings started and the angry blood began pounding. She tried to halt the downward plunge with something tedious and debilitating: looking at the week's televisions programmes or washing and chopping the vegetables for a ratatouille, or if Mrs Mac were still there prodding her into one of her boring monologues.

Ups and downs followed hard on each other at this time, at the start of Noel's Den. Their coming took her by surprise, they were hard to control. It was darling Noel woven into everything, into his absence as into his presence.

But always when Noel got home, and in those days the hour was reasonable, Geraldine was smiling and ready with her love. She listened to his stories of the day's events, saying nothing, maybe just a comment or two on grating voices, or somebody's piggish way of eating, or the poisonous body odour of some pretty girl luncher.

Geraldine sat forward. They'd stopped. It was still raining. Noel was smiling at her, turned towards her with an arm on the steering-wheel. Warm brown eyes with two perpendicular worry lines between them, fine dark eyebrows, the tilted smile, his darling teeth, smooth tanned skin, lovely virile ears, narrow nose. The beginnings of dissipation.

She burrowed against him with her head on his shoulder. 'Are we here?'

———

CHAPTER 3

'It's a pub, angel, Don wants a drink. Not much further, though.'

It seemed like the middle of the night. It looked an awful place. She saw Julie and Bernard going in. Don must be in there already.

'We don't want one, do we?'

Noel grinned. She thought it might work, the bracketing them together, just for a moment she thought Noel would stay with her.

'Jesus, goddess, a night like this and that godawful drive – come on and get stuck in.'

Geraldine sighed, then smiled. She made Noel put on his mac. Then together, holding hands, they ran through the rain. She could go to the lavatory now instead of putting it off until Murwillumbah.

A poisonous interior, gloomy with old dark paint. A wet middle-aged woman drinking alone at one side of the jutting bar, three leering dirty men at the other, a greasy glass display of bright yellow cake, an upright dusty piano. Julie was already chatting up the publican, a tall, morose-looking man with black hair that spread from the centre in two flat curves on his forehead. It was at Julie the men were leering, and now their eyes took in Geraldine too. The publican jerked a thumb when Geraldine asked for the lavatory. Noel had joined Don and Bernard at a pinball machine. Halfway up a dark staircase the Queen hung lopsided in colour. The passage was even dimmer than the bar. Geraldine found the lavatory by its smell but could find no light switch. With the aid of her tissues, and standing up, she managed without touching anything. Even the old-fashioned chain she pulled without contact. The Hotel Champion, the end of the world. She wouldn't be disheartened. There was nowhere to wash her hands.

Back in the bar she used a pre-moist towel from her bag. They were all drinking schooners of beer, Don and Bernard just starting on their second. Julie had joined the three dirty men; she was laughing and egging them on. The wet woman hadn't moved, moody with sherry. Geraldine couldn't sit down or even lean on the slimy surfaces. She didn't drink. But she mustn't get depressed. It worried Noel when she was depressed. It was in her own interests to stay cheerful and tolerant, because Noel had to be shocked into recollection of the Geraldine he'd been drifting from.

The pinball machine was hilarious. Noel was very matey with Don and Bernard. His easy adaptability.

Geraldine touched Noel's arm. 'I'll wait in the Land-Rover.'

'Okay, angel, shan't be long.' Not even turning his head.

Geraldine took off her raincoat and got in, then shook the raincoat out the door and draped it to dry in the back. It wouldn't dry, and it was hard not to cry at the thought of pitching camp in all this rain in the dark unknown quantity of Murwillumbah. Everything got mucky in this weather. Did Don know where he was heading? A sign on a post in the pub's evil yellow light said Brunswick Heads. Geraldine got out the map. They were nearly there. But where was there?

It seemed hours before they came out noisy and laughing and calling back beery cheerios to those inside. Noel was holding Julie's arm, perhaps just to keep her steady. She saw him toss his cigarette away before going round the Land-Rover.

'Pushing on to Brisbane, goddess.' Noel said getting in with gusts of beery breath. 'The locals say it's fine there.' He started up after Don who was already moving.

'What's fine?'

'Weather, silly. Must say I agree with Don, don't you?'

'Of course, darling.'

Her words sounded sardonic. In trying to keep the bleakness she felt from her voice, the sarcastic note had crept in. She hoped Noel hadn't noticed. She wanted to touch him but somehow couldn't. Just stroke his arm. She couldn't. She wanted to say something, anything, something flippant and light, any old casual comment. She huddled into her corner.

Noel didn't speak. They were both tired. They'd been on the road about twelve hours. Tweed Heads went by, then Coolangatta, then Surfers Paradise all aglitter with dreadful gaiety. Geraldine shut her eyes, willing her mind to shut too. She could tell when they got to Brisbane by the stopping and starting and cornering, by the noises and lights. Then a longer stop and Geraldine could see Don in some place, no doubt making enquiries. Then they started up again. She glanced at Noel once and saw a little smile. What did Noel have to smile about? Something she didn't have?

I must fight this depression.

At last they drove through sagging gates to the bleakest place on earth. Geraldine got out and stretched. It was a fine starry night with the moon shining down on hundreds of transients moving among their caravans and tents. Hanging lanterns bobbled about beneath the sparse dim gloom of the official lighting. Here and there torches moved over the ground or ran over the tents. A dog barked somewhere and a child started wailing.

Geraldine set to work with the others. She found the exertion rewarding. Weights that made Julie pant and gasp Geraldine took in her stride. She'd never pitched a tent in her life but followed Noel's instructions without a hitch and they had their two tents up in no time.

'No need for you to do this, angel.'

'I'm loving every moment.' Quickly she kissed his cheek.

She caught Don's admiring look. She was suddenly exultant. The down was gone, the up back in place. Ridiculous to be unbalanced by a few drops of rain and a smelly loo. This was Brisbane, the planned turning-point. She had the funny feeling stronger than ever: after Brisbane they'd reach the precious truth. She took one of the big plastic drums and filled it with water at the community taps then carried it back. Don saw her coming and rushed to help.

'Hey, no need for that, water's laid on.'

'Nice to have them ready for tomorrow.' Geraldine smiled.

'You little beauty,' Don said admiringly, and wouldn't let her take the second one. Masterfully he took it himself. What a nice face he had, broad and strong and twinkly.

When Julie suggested a break to eat, it was Geraldine who said, 'Let's get everything organised first.'

Even Julie's admiration was plain, and Bernard said, 'Glutton for punishment when you get going.'

They'd been in two minds about her, and now they felt that she'd come good after all. There was no stopping her until their camp was shipshape. It was a good impression to make and it was well calculated to make a good impression. With a fixed smile she watched Julie making her stew with hanging hair and unwashed hands, and said gaily, 'How about that damper?'

'Gosh,' Julie said, 'not a hope, maybe tomorrow night.'

'We won't let her get out of it, will we, darling?' Geraldine took Noel's hand and held it in the romantic light from the fire in the dirty old open concrete fireplace, one of several provided in the park. Noel pressed her fingers, caressing each in turn. He looked relaxed and happy. Geraldine had Kraft cheese and biscuits and an apple, sighing that despite its scrumptious smell she was too tired for stew.

They were all dead beat, talking little and yawning a lot.

Don apologised for the long day, blaming the rain. Nearly 600 kilometres. Julie and Bernard whipped through the washing-up, then Bernard said goodnight and went into his tent. Then Julie, then Don.

'Good night, you lovebirds,' Don said with a naked leer. Geraldine loved it.

'Come on, goddess, I'm all in, you must be too.'

She followed Noel to his tent. He turned there and kissed her. 'Have a good sleep, goddess, I'm dead already. Got everything you need?'

'Yes, thank you.' Noel's tent flap closed. No, I need you. She stared at Noel's flap and turned suddenly. Everything you need. She went into her tent. The orange canvas. Everything you need. Hateful, hateful people. The bleakest place on earth.

Everything you need. The comfort of Noel's arms. That was all. Just the comfort of Noel's arms. No more, nothing else because all the stretchers creaked. Just comfort in his arms.

———

CHAPTER 4

Park was an optimistic term for the dreary expanse. Its name on a dirty board was Water View. No water, just some straggly gums struggling from the worn dusty ground. Dozens of caravans, each with its tent and a bawling kid or two and line of washing. A concrete block of showers and lavatories. A lot of dark-skinned people, the men showy with long black lustrous hair, the women slatternly in taffeta and voile and rampant maternity. Geraldine heard Don tell Julie they were Romany gypsies, circus people in Queensland for winter show time. In summer they'd do the southern circuit. Geraldine squashed a lot of ants, but surreptitiously, because Noel was funny about killing things.

Noel was busy with the others, striking camp. Geraldine stayed aloof this morning.

In the early months of marriage Noel had asked, 'Any kids on the programme?'

'We'll see.' Geraldine would never share him with a child. 'If you really want one, darling, though they do say the world's dangerously over-populated.'

'The world can go stuff itself as far as my kid's concerned.' He smiled the heartstrings-tugger. 'Give you something else to fuss over.'

'I don't fuss,' Geraldine said, smiling and straightening his polo neck.

'A fussy old hen,' Noel said, giving her a hug. Geraldine

returned his hug. In those days she did, always, unquestion-
ingly. That strings were now attached was Noel's doing.

On the way out of Brisbane they stopped at the Land-
Rover depot, then again for provisions. Geraldine took no part
in these trifling activities, and in any case was too disheartened
this morning. She sat drumming her fingers on her knee and
watched Noel involving himself with the others. It all took an
age. More stuff was jammed in the back of their Land-Rover.

Just over four years ago Noel had a vasectomy. Geraldine
talked him into it; she said it was morally right. It was during
the worst period of his rat-race grizzles, and Noel went off in
a temper to have it done as if this were one more imposition
on him of the whole rotten bloody system. But it remained a
grudge inside him, Geraldine knew by the puns he made
solely and privately for her discomfiture. 'Ask my wife,' he'd
say to Dennis regarding one of their *plats du jour*, 'she knows
an excellent short cut,' and raise a quizzical eyebrow for
Geraldine's benefit. Or if Clyde or someone got drunkenly
quarrelsome at one of Noel's parties Noel would look straight
at her with a bland smile and say, 'Cut it out, old man.'

Noel got back in the Land-Rover. 'Off we go, angel –
excited?' He waited for Don to move then fell in behind.
Geraldine squeezed his thigh, saying nothing, not wanting to
show her melancholy.

But when they were beyond the city and she saw the
Glasshouse Mountains rising stark from the flat her spirits
soared too. It would be soon now, perhaps tonight at their
next camp. The map showed a thinning-out of places; more of
space and less of people the further north they went. Noel
looked happier today, as if he too were closer to some goal.
Could it be the same? How funny, how delicious, if Noel had
seized on this trip because he too wanted to stop their drift.
He'd known she'd come too, deep down. How lovable he was.
She remembered instances of his thoughtfulness. She always
tried not to over-criticise because of the special way he had of
looking abashed and accepting her rebukes, and then doing

something nice for her or buying her some little thoughtful gift. Noel was crazy for her, there was no doubt. And such a darling, they all said so. His friends told Geraldine she was lucky to have Noel. Geraldine thought so too and thought he was equally lucky in having her and wondered if his friends told him how lucky he was.

They passed through a pleasant town called Nambour with friendly signs saying Welcome and Come Again. Beyond Noel Geraldine saw Noosa Heads loom up impressively from the ocean's edge. They were making a steady pace through pretty country, a dairying district of hills and valleys with cultivated fields, and further inland the dark bulk of timber. The cold of morning had gone, the sun sparkled, not a cloud in sight.

'Yes,' she said with a smile.

'Yes what?'

'Yes, I'm excited.'

'Good for you.' Noel threw her a grin. 'Nice change from the daily grind.'

'We'll make it all different now,' Geraldine said in a soft voice. 'I mean after this.'

It was a long time before Noel said, 'One thing it's got to be is different.' There was a change in his voice, and Geraldine saw yesterday's frown was back.

He meant conditions at Noel's Den, poor darling. They could engage a manager, they could afford it. She'd suggest it. He could ease up then, spend more time with her. Take something up, he was always talking about it. She smoothed down his too-long hair at the back.

Noel jerked his head. 'Stop fussing.'

Geraldine snatched her hand away. It would never do to upset things now with the reconciliation so close.

Just beyond Gympie there was a lot of sugar. The sun beat down on the cane and the cane closed in, stifling and sticky.

It was only when his own faults troubled his conscience that Noel said she fussed. But they'd forget all that, wipe the

slate clean. She imagined their homecoming, a new start, saw
Noel in her house. But a changed Noel, a Noel with time to
love, as eager as she to hold tight to what they had.

The cane looked full of snakes and leeches and lemmings,
the green tops deceptive. Underneath it was all thick foetid
stems, brownish and mucky like treacle.

Noel fell in love with her house too. Biggish, in
Woollahra, white, verandahs upstairs, a glassed-in patio downstairs, a big front garden and a lane at the back. The new carport off the patio had access from back and front. The new
pool was behind the house so Geraldine could swim in privacy. As soon as her mother died Geraldine made improvements, got rid of a lot of old stuff that held the imprint of both
parents, but especially her father in his conservative suits and
pretence of frowning probity. New clever furniture. Then
Andrew had done some wonderful things under her direction,
all sorts of built-ins. A super kitchen, running like clockwork
behind its relaxed air. Andrew was always around touching
things up and suggesting others, or at least he used to be. Poor
Andrew, making do with Gail.

'Tired, darling?' she asked. Oh God, I love you.

Noel shrugged.

She pressed close. 'I'm sorry, darling, about your hair, I
didn't mean to fuss.' Automatically she adjusted the neck of his
T-shirt. Noel's frown came back, and a sort of tension.
Geraldine withdrew to her side and watched the road fly past.
Patches of sugar burning. Blasts of heat.

Don kept on past Maryborough before stopping for lunch.
Men were all the same in cars, once started that was enough.
It was going to be another long day.

After lunch Geraldine lost count of time. They crossed a
river called Isis and went through a town called Childers: great
dark trees, Victorian facades, timber and columns and lacy
balconies. A quick stop for petrol, pees, bad news in the paper
and tea in their Thermoses. Then on again through Gin Gin,
midget memorial soldier on a massive plinth. Flowering trees

in pink and white, wattles with long yellow blossoms, all blur-
ring past.

On a hot journey the smell of yourself is sickening.

Geraldine took her shoes off, then her socks. A tiny
motel called the Colosseum whizzed by. They could go
abroad. Noel would like that: Rome, the Colosseum, gal-
leries and churches full of goddesses and angels. It would be
all this driving making him edgy. He loved her to nestle
against him. She'd perfected the air of childlike dependence
because it tickled Noel; his maleness liked it. 'Such a surprise in a great big girl like you,' he'd tease, or call her his
dear little dinosaur.

'You staying in there all night, angel?' Noel had her door
open and his face was laughing in at her. Geraldine saw the
others already at work. It seemed in the dark in a pleasant flat
place of trees and grass. 'You were miles away,' Noel said.

'Where are we?'

'Just beyond Miriam Vale.' He went then, round to let
down the back and get busy with the others. Geraldine
checked on the map, over 500 kilometres. It was the wrong
place for reasoning and reconciliation. Wrong in Land-
Rovers. A between-time was best, the overnight quiet.

Could this be the place? Torches swept the flat ground
and kerosene lanterns made moving pools of light.
Geraldine took torch and lavatory roll to a big tree far
enough away to pee safely behind. Then back in the Land-
Rover she took her shoes off again and shut her eyes, slump-
ing back. She felt filthy.

It took a big effort to rouse herself, to join the others and
smile and lend a hand, then to get water in her plastic bowl
and wash herself bits at a time on the other side of their
Land-Rover. But worth it. Deodorised and talcumed she
could sit on her groundsheet at the campfire and smile at
unwashed Julie stirring her witch's brew.

'Bernard's eyes were on Geraldine's feet,' 'Ought to put
your shoes on,' he said, 'spiders and scorpions.'

'Stamp out bare feet.' Don bellowed with laughter in the same pink shirt. Noel joined in. Geraldine too.

Noel got her shoes and socks from the Land-Rover.

'No damper, Julie?' Geraldine grinned like everybody grinned.

'Gosh, you can blame Don for that,' Julie said, tossing her hair back without moving back from the pot. 'I bet that's why he keeps going so late, he's dreading my damper.'

Don gave her a hearty slap on the bottom. He was in high spirits, without a singlet, the pink shirt open to reveal his hairy chest that went into rolls of fat lower down.

Noel had a nice body, taut still despite the wine. Save Noel's body along with the rest of him. She saw him running downstairs at home. She was always frightened he'd slip. The morning they'd left, Noel running down; the house, quiet, calm, empty but for themselves. As usual she was ready first and went out into the garden in her rubber-soled boots and looked at the white house so clearly visible in the chill and frosty dark. But Geraldine's vision was never dependent on light, it was their sole and quiet possession of it she saw. This was the way it would be when they came back. She remembered tugging the black woolly cap down over her ears and laughing in exultation. They hadn't got away till after lunch, spoiling things. But she remembered the early mood; she was up there now on the same exalted plane.

'Come back, angel, down with us ordinary folks. Grub's ready.' Noel was laughing as he ladled great helpings from Julie's pot into their dixies. 'She gets these bouts,' he told the others, 'soars off alone somewhere way out of reach.' Oh, Noel! Silly Noel!

Geraldine pushed the stew around in the dixie. Julie had managed rice too. Mrs Mac was going to pop in every day at the house to be on what she called the safe side. Geraldine liked Mrs Mac's proprietary interest; it paid to pay well. Julie was eyeing her uneaten food so Geraldine took a big breath and plunged, shutting her senses off till it was all gone. The same with the poisonous coffee. Don cracked some macadamia nuts cleverly with two axes, and Geraldine shared the remains of her Kraft and the two avocadoes she'd hoarded.

There was no wind, a crescent moon coming and going between wisps of cloud and the feeling of dew in the air. They sat about for a while, enjoying the quiet. Julie was first to move, then Bernard got a grip on Geraldine to help her up. She snatched her arm away. Noel laughed to make light of it and said, 'Doesn't like contact, old man.' Making it worse, making them all look.

Geraldine washed up and Julie dried. Geraldine could feel Bernard's eyes on her from where he sat in the dark beyond the camp fire. Noel had made a thing of a little quirk that should have passed unnoticed. She supposed he was trying to fit in with these strange people who were not their kind of people. It didn't matter; it didn't affect the real issue. She was glad now they'd kept going; Don had planned to stop just beyond Childers, but they'd all wanted to go on, Don too, just as if they *all* had some special goal. It amused Geraldine.

They turned in early. Noel pecked her goodnight and that was all, they went to their separate tents. But Geraldine was still on a cloud, above the trivialities of Julie's food and Bernard's touch and Noel's disloyal laughter. Things that flew off and vanished. She fell asleep almost at once.

It was dark when she awoke. In the torchlight her watch said nearly five. Every cog of her body felt at ease, smooth and functioning, and it was up in her head too: a slow woozy sense of peace and well-being so rare of late it was almost forgotten. Unfrantic. She recognised it as the power she had of setting herself aloof, free in the highest sense from the inconsistencies that bugged ordinary people. She got up and dressed quickly and went outside. No torch. The dark was light enough. How lovely it was. Geraldine strolled slowly away from the tents, rambling among the trees. The sky would soon wake to life. The birds knew, rustling and twittering. There were wild tree orchids high on some of the trunks. Under the trees the grass was soft and fine and soaked with dew. A smell of wet leaves, now and then a fugitive scent, perhaps shy bush flowers. A slight wind stirring, the air rousing itself through its mantle of dew. Her heavy boots were sopping, but inside her feet were dry. The air was a caress, and up through the feathery heights of the trees soft pale colours were starting, the only things alive herself and the bush with all its secret dwellers. Little twigs uplifted in happiness. Twigs beneath her feet crackling, the wind's whisper, the whistling note of a bird, the strident cackle of another. It was growing lighter; the dark was going. Noel must feel the same. Perhaps he was awake. It was wrong to sleep through this dawning. Geraldine turned back. Somebody was moving in the camp. She hurried.

It was Bernard. He gave her a furtive look and a wide berth, then a morning growl of acknowledgement.

They set off at seven-thirty. During breakfast a different wind got up and flooded the campsite with a smell of evil.

'Dead cow, probably,' Don said.

Geraldine clung to her mood. Noel seemed smoothed out, the frown gone. A sign on the road, Children Cross, made him laugh.

'Good idea,' he said. 'let's all have 'em; Noel cross, Geraldine cross. Pin 'em on so people leave you alone,'

Geraldine laughed too.

Just before Rockhampton a lot of purple and pink Bougainvillaea wound among trees in yellow fields of grass. Cattle stood about. The grass was long, thick, pale and silky. Rockhampton's neat and ordered look appealed to the order in Geraldine's mind. She liked its wide streets, solid buildings, the broad River Fitzroy, the bridge over the railway. The day was lovely as dawn had promised, and the jets of a fountain tossed diamonds into the sunshine. Geraldine drew a rapturous sigh, but kept to her side of the Land-Rover, fearful of fracturing Noel's fragile good temper.

Leafy little trees grew by the road with single yellow flowers like wild roses.

They stopped early for lunch at a muddy creek. Julie wiped the sharp all-purpose knife on her filthy jeans before slicing salami. Geraldine shut her eyes and thought of beauty. The tea was thick, dark and soupy, made from bore water out of a tap there.

'Hold your breath it tastes like nectar,' Noel said, making a funny face.

Geraldine had two Ryvitas out of her private tin. They all watched.

'She's a cut above,' Noel said with one of his bland vasectomy smiles. Why must he keep on and on with it?

All in a moment Geraldine hated everything. Dirt and heat. Their hands. Julie's knife. Tents. Scanty ablutions in chancy privacy, stale repetitive talk, worn-out jokes, smoky fires, dirty clothes, Noel's puns, the same faces. She'd seen Julie wash her face once, the men never. Tiring chores. Needless privations. Water. She felt a spurt of anger against Noel. A pointless journey that Geraldine must give point to. The spartan element would worsen as they went north, the privations become obligatory. Just because silly Noel liked to be liked; even these strangers he sought to please. She was the exception, and must remain the balanced one, rational as always, the last to reach breaking-point.

'I'll do it, Julie.' Noel's voice, and Geraldine looked up to watch him take the billy from Julie and go to the tap. He rinsed it.

'Wishing you hadn't come?' Don dropped down beside her, still pink but a deeper shade and the hairy gross torso and great hairy legs that came out of brief shorts.

'Not at all,' Geraldine said, 'I'm loving it.'

'Just get the feeling you don't fit in.' Don's eyes were kind in his coarse face. She knew the look, the desire that lay at the back of it.

Noel was coming. Geraldine gave Don her brilliant warm

smile. 'You're quite wrong, it's a wonderful experience. If you mean food, it's just I have a small appetite.'

'Eats like a horse at home,' Noel said. Noel, who was never at home. His hand on her hair, the quizzical look down at her. 'We're not cut out for roughing it, are we, angel?' Keeping on.

Geraldine slid from his touch, making it part of getting up. 'Let's move on, shall we?' She began helping Julie. She heard a silence behind her and felt the emptiness start: Noel would slip away again. He could smile and joke with these people, laugh at their hackneyed humour. The reverse of the frowns he kept for her. She was sick with foreboding. What had happened? Nothing had changed: she was the same goddess he'd loved all along.

It was hilly country then. And masses of wattle suddenly up a rise, a cloud of yellow, each flower long like a catkin.

'D'you like these people, darling, really and truly?'

'They're okay.'

'They're dull though, aren't they, and dirty.'

'Christ, they're just human.'

She'd meant to keep her mouth shut. It puzzled her that Noel was so prickly. Just with her.

Distance was all around them, in front and rushing past and growing longer behind. It was inside with them too. It doesn't count. Say that, keep saying it: all this doesn't count. Make the best of even the worst of it. In the long run she'd thank these poisonous people. She drew close to Noel, resting her cheek a moment on his shoulder; but only a moment because of the jolts.

In the fading light there were rolling downs, dark trees dotted on the pale grass, evenly sprinkled as if by a measuring hand.

They camped near nowhere, halfway between Rockhampton and Mackay. Another 400 kilometres nearer the point. Their fifth camp.

———

CHAPTER 5

Was there some significance about the morning? There was Noel's lighthearted mood. There was his loving manner with its hint of compunction. Perhaps he'd done some thinking in his orange tent, on the squeaking stretcher. Perhaps this would be the day. The map looked nice. Soon they'd see the start of Barrier Reef islands, there'd be more quiet to talk in.

They drove up from the valley. The mists below were sun-lit and lovely: motionless pockets, wisps and scarves wreathing away lazily. Geraldine thought when she got back to Sydney she'd continue with early rising. It gave one a grip on the day.

A black cat dead on the road. Cattle country but dull, a straight road through uniform dull grey bush. Two dead walla-bies. It often happened at night, people said; it was a chance they took. The road kept on. It was hard to remember that over any hill there might be beauty. At times it seemed pointless, cover-ing distance, travelling to no purpose, purposelessly tired. A progression and yet none. Noel near. Noel far. Four enormous cactuses. Then mango trees in bloom, shapely bushy blobs of burnished pink. Through Mackay, quaint silly buildings. A misty sort of haze over the sea, the shallows starting. Glimpses of islands. The strong sun, the sweat, clothes sticking. Noel in shorts beside her, his thin brown legs showing sinews.

'You've gone away again, goddess.'

'No, darling, I'm here.' She touched his leg and let her hand stay. She smiled at him.

She felt their closeness. She didn't notice lunch and could never afterwards remember whether they'd had any that day. Just out of Proserpine, long-stemmed mauve lilies grew in a stream called Lethe Brook. Oblivion for the past, such trifling differences, then a fresh start together.

They camped that night at Bowen. Don's crinkly eyes on her over a dinner of chops and sausages Julie had got at Mackay. She would always remember Don's crinkly eyes because, looking back, they seemed full of a knowledge she didn't have.

The mood that night was jovial. Noel had the most whisky and kept Don and Julie in stitches. Even Bernard smiled at Noel's stories and his crazy mimicry. Geraldine too. Then Noel and Don washed up.

Noel's goodnight kiss was very sweet. It wasn't the whisky; it was far too real. They weren't in sight of the others. He hugged her close. His face was bristly. 'Sleep well, Geraldine.' He gave her a friendly pat, like a dog.

'Can I come in?' she asked softly. Noel was going into his tent. He turned his head. 'It won't take you long to shave,' she added, and at once wished the words back.

But Noel didn't flare up. Instead he took her in his arms roughly, as Don might, and kissed her so violently her face was stung by his. 'Not tonight, angel,' he said with a funny smile, 'but bear it in mind.'

Geraldine went to her orange tent on a cloud. There was absolutely no warning. Unless it was calling her Geraldine.

No warning, none at all.

At breakfast, during cold sausages, Julie had a feeling in her bones that tonight would be damper night.

'Count me out,' Noel said.

'I thought you were panting for a damper,' Julie teased.

'It's not the damper, it's just I won't be around.'

None of them got his meaning, especially Geraldine.

'Banquet date somewhere?' Don guffawed at his own wit.

Noel smiled. 'Just going back,' he said, 'okay?'

It didn't sink in.

'Sure, mate, just as you like,' Don said affably, 'we agreed to no compulsion.'

It was one of his jokes.

'We'll work out a refund,' Don said, 'hire of the vehicles etcetera.'

'Come off it.' Noel stood up with his mug of coffee. 'A few dollars.'

'We'll miss you,' Julie said, 'I bet it's the damper, you just can't face it.'

Everyone was so calm, so ordinary.

Then Bernard said, 'Gerry going along too, I suppose?'

Noel shrugged. 'It's up to her – well, see you all later. I'd better pack my gear.' He moved off casually towards his tent with the mug.

Casually.

Geraldine felt their eyes. She couldn't look at them. She got up and went after Noel at an easy pace, it was in her mind that she ran. She went in.

'What's the matter?'

'Just going back, that's all.'

'But why?'

He looked at her. 'The same old thing.'

'Why?'

'You know why. If you don't know now you'll never know.'

'How could I know? Tell me.' She felt a great hollow inside.

'Because you're obsessed, you never let up. Look, angel, we've had it all out before, for all the good it's done. Your insane possessive jealousy, your bloody moods – why d'you think I jumped at this trip, just to get away? Do some thinking, take stock.'

Take stock, that was rich. 'Didn't you want me to come?'

'Hell, no.'

Geraldine felt him slide away, and desperation was greater

than the anger she felt at his brutal and vulgar denial of her. 'But what's the matter? Is it being married? Would you like a divorce and then just live together?'

Noel looked smiling and bored and began shoving clothes into his seabag.

Geraldine sat down on the edge of his stretcher, deaf to its groan. 'But you were so thrilled at me coming.'

'Was I?' Noel's voice was low and savage. He hurled some tan shorts on the ground. 'There was just no way – I couldn't stand another one of your fits.'

Fits. Geraldine was too choked to speak.

'It's hounded me from the start,' Noel said. 'Every move I make you're on the watch, all the time, fussing and fiddling and interfering, all that bloody smooching. Running my life – well, no more.'

How funny in a little tent. 'Why suddenly here?'

Noel looked at her in perplexity. 'This is what gets me – this pretence it's sudden, as though it's never arisen.' His face softened and he went down on his haunches in front of her. 'It's driving me dotty, goddess – it's Dennis one day, Elaine the next, or it's the Den or Clyde, now Julie, anything to feed your crazy jealousy. There's a great big world going on all around and you don't even know it's there.'

The world, as if she cared. She looked at his dear face through a blur of tears. 'I haven't said a word since we left Sydney.'

'You don't need to now, you say it all in silence.' He got up and went back to his packing.

Geraldine remembered something. Anger was starting. 'The third day of our honeymoon – don't tell me my jealousy made you sneak off on the third day of our honeymoon, the whole day?'

Noel paused in what he was doing and looked at her. 'Yes, since I was stifled to death already.'

'Not too stifled to enjoy my income.'

'Jesus, yes, that bloody income too.'

Geraldine looked at her fingers twisting together. She couldn't see what Noel was getting at. The impotence of his arguments was pathetic, he had no case. Or was lying. 'Please, Noel,' she said, not moving, not looking at him, 'let's be rational and honest, you're just tired of the trip, aren't you? You just can't see a thing through, your job, your first marriage, this trip. Now you want to drag *our* marriage in.' When Noel was silent she added, 'Suppose I said I'd come back too?'

'Just as you like; it makes no difference.'

She looked at him then. 'We'll make it work, darling, let's *both* try. That was the point – getting away. I came to take stock too – both of us together, I've been waiting for the right time and place, I didn't know -' I didn't know you hated me.

Noel was kneading a pair of socks. 'There's no point, angel.' He hurled the ball into his seabag.

They'd kept their voices low. This was no affair of the others.

'Please, Noel.' She had to plea. 'Stay – please, darling – we'll thrash it out, you're wrong to say I'm jealous. When have I ever been jealous?'

Noel laughed – not a nice sound. 'You're so full of bloody delusions; that's just another about hiding your jealousy.' He lit a cigarette and looked at her with the blank smile she hated. 'Why d'you think I practically live at the Den, scarcely come home, fill up the house with people when I do?' Geraldine stared back. 'Just for peace and quiet away from you.'

It was all too pat. Too bland. He was too bland not to be lying. He used none of the shifts and dodges of truth.

'I think I deserve the truth,' Geraldine said.

Noel turned in contempt, rested his cigarette and resumed packing. 'You've got the truth.'

It was his manner, not his words, that incensed Geraldine. She jumped up from the stretcher. 'It's Dennis, isn't it; that's the truth?'

'Don't screech,' Noel said.

Geraldine rushed at him, but Noel turned in time and caught her raised arms. 'You never loved me, you were always slippery, right from the first on our honeymoon – '

'Keep you voice down – Christ, don't put on one of your turns.'

Geraldine wrenched away. Her eyes felt starting from her head and she could hear funny little moans. There was so much she had to say: accusations, pleas, loving words, the truth, make him listen to the truth, poor darling Noel, make him, make him – and do: hurt, scratch, love, kiss, wound and console, explain, yes, explain to Noel about death and how sometimes she saw it and it was in a smell or a slither or a whisper or a sly look or an ultimatum and make him see that without him she could have no life, she would be dead, at death's mercy, dead, his body hers, he was hers, she was in his arms, his arms round her, holding, hurting.

'You need treatment,' Noel's voice said.

Geraldine laughed. 'Such a little thing, less than nothing, darling.'

'You're not making sense, you'd better lie down a while.'

'Don't touch me,' she shouted, 'don't touch me.'

Noel's arms dropped. 'Just as you like.'

The floor of the tent was earth. Noel had the same floor of stunted grass she had in her tent. Everything in her body felt rigid. Even her eyes, a jerk up. The same slanting walls of orange canvas. The house he filled up was *her* house. 'When are you leaving?'

Noel's voice shrugged. 'Don't know. There's transport to look into. You coming back with me?'

Geraldine smiled from the tent flap. 'I don't give up so easily.'

'Good for you.'

Don was still by the dying fire, smoking. Julie and Bernard had gone for a look-see at Bowen, he said. Geraldine sat down near him and smiled and asked him about his job, and Don told her about interstate haulage and kept asking what was so funny because of Geraldine's smile.

If he'd met someone else, fallen in love, it would be different, she'd understand. But she hadn't dared say this, hadn't dared put the idea into his head.

She broke into one of Don's anecdotes. 'I'm coming on with you. D'you think we'll reach Cairns tomorrow?'

Don stared a moment then looked away. 'I guess, if we start early.'

'Let's start early.'

She stayed in her tent most of the day, in the hot unbearable orange.

CHAPTER 6

Camp 6. Bowen. A salt works. They could have her tears. Bleak and desolate, dead. Dry creeks and rivers. Bowen: never remembered but unforgotten. She didn't see Noel again. He wasn't there next morning when they left. In just six days and nights Noel had slipped away from her. He'd played dirty. The weather hot and humid, the ground parched. A salt works.

———

CHAPTER 7

Geraldine's spirits rose with the movement forward, going towards the goal. Don was driving, Bernard and Julie in the other. Four was better, two apiece. Don's hands instead of Noel's. Broad, strong, fattish with freckles. Behind and seawards the Whitsunday Passage with the hazed, bushy islands beyond: Hayman, Hook, Whitsunday.

The scenery got better with Noel gone. Don was amused at Upstart Bay. It was nice chatting to Don, somebody who meant nothing, laughing at the way he called everything a bugger: a dip in the road, a hitch-hiking blowfly, dust, sun, sweat, a road bend, motor-bikes. St Stephen's Greek Orthodox Church, blue and white with a little belfry. A very long beautiful iron bridge between Home Hill and Ayr, across the Burdekin River. Supplies and pees. Looking into distances is good for one's eyes, Don said. And no city worries away up here. A strange weatherboard church, high and narrow. Everything had significance. Steps flying up to stilt houses. Great Northern Hotel. Slender columns of a stone church.

Geraldine found Don amusing, a good companion, Even his small discoloured teeth. How Noel would laugh when she told him Don's asides. Dear Noel had some business upset and was determined to spare her, the darling.

All that day she was on a high. The movement forward, the going on. Chatting to Don, laughing at his truck driver's ready wit that was as new to her as the landscape. It couldn't be true, it was absurd, crazy – herself and an interstate haulier on the way to the point she'd meant to reach with Noel. She laughed aloud, and Don's twinkly smile joined in.

Don was hell-bent on reaching Cairns, saying she'd challenged him. It became a game. It grew to a lovely blue. They whizzed along, and now the significance lay in getting there. Townsville was just a place where they got petrol, where Don was impatient with Bernard for lagging, and Bernard didn't reply, looking sulky, and Julie asked Don if the cops were after him. Bernard was just as morose at Ingham, where lunch was on a check tablecloth in a nice little café. Then a lot of that terribly funny sugar again and off the coast the islands of the Great Barrier Reef. It was a heady day, cut adrift as she was and yet somehow with the strongest grip on the future. It wasn't she who'd given up, and the thought was intoxicating.

They passed a cinema called Sugarama and a signpost pointing to El Arish. And Don said Innisfail's blackened buildings came from being built of burnt sugar. It was all hilarious. So was the dark when they got to Cairns. They'd done just on 600 kilometres, the longest day yet. That was a scream too and Bernard's snarling gloom, and the fact that it was far too late for camping and all five dozen motels were full. And the man at the Land-Rover depot's face saying Cairns was always full in the season, and his phoning around till he got them squashed in at a ramshackle weatherboard pile called the Buona Vista Private Hotel. Geraldine collapsed in giggles at the dark poky rooms half filled by leaning lugubrious wardrobes. She shared a room with Julie, even a bed. All night long there were feet and cisterns and doors and snoring, Julie said, at daybreak, but Geraldine was dead with the exhaustion she'd wanted and heard nothing of this.

The storm was close next morning. Perhaps the two men had shipped it along overnight. The camping-site at a beach outside Cairns seemed a sore point between them. The explosion came at lunch-time, over such a trifle; over Bernard overdoing the scrambled eggs.

'For God's sake!' Don knocked him aside.

'What the hell!' Bernard snarled. Then, with a menacing grip on the spoon, 'You'd better watch it, mate.'

Julie raised an eyebrow at Geraldine and smiled. But Geraldine didn't smile.

'For Chris'sake it's simple enough scrambling eggs.'

'Get stuffed,' Bernard shouted. 'Scramble your own bloody eggs. Who paid for the shitting things, anyway?'

Words she didn't want to hear: vulgar words, foul, trite. Geraldine shut her ears. People everywhere, a falling off. Noel not measuring up –

'That bloody camera.'

'What's the rush, anyhow? This was to be an easy trip, a holiday.'

A holiday. The chilling sense of emptiness. Noel gone.

Things she wouldn't listen to. Clyde saying – what was Clyde saying? Shouting? 'What about expenses? Share and share alike, you said. So far I've paid for bloody everything.' No, not Clyde, who talked in abstracts of yield, takeover, upswing, trend, property and combine. Noel paid for everything. Dennis had his head screwed on the right way. Noel paid, no worries about the screw of his head because of her money behind him.

Stray words. Somebody shouting. 'Who gave you the right to set the pace?' That was Bernard, a pale voice full of resentment.

'What's bloody eating *you?* You're mad, yer bugger. The front vehicle sets the pace.'

The voices impinged on their life together. All because Noel had to be bolstered by an audience. Geraldine went out of her way to accommodate his friends, a compensation for hating them so. One would think her fortitude must show. A helpful, hostessy face till they were gone. And always so nice in rebuking him. She wanted Noel to herself; it wasn't too much to ask. It was cruel of him to make her share him with others. Ordinary, dull, meretricious. She tried to tell him this, gently and understandingly, but Noel just laughed and said, 'Everyone's ordinary, us too, nothing so special about us, is there?' With a loving embrace. Poor Noel. Hopeless even trying to point out to him the specialness of their love, of him, her, their marriage: not as a bit of paper but as a whole coming together. If only he'd equalled her image of him they would be so happy. Noel was four years older but, tragically, so immature. Growing up in the wrong home with the wrong clothes and hair. Even on their one free day a week since Noel's Den started, Sunday, he got his hordes of sycophants flocking into her house. Every Sunday, no respite. Even around her swimming-pool.

Geraldine tried to shut her ears but couldn't escape their voices.

'For one thing you can take that bloody drum of flour I'm stuck with. The rate we're gong there's no chance of a damper.'

'For God's sake pipe down, you want the whole world to know?'

'Just because Blaine took a powder and we're stuck with his fucking wife – '

The breaking-up, the disintegration. The long deterioration then – crash. The inevitable downsliding. Hadn't it always been like that? Instability, shouts and curses, Noel's conscience at war with his folly and lack of judgement. She could never make Noel see his silliness, he didn't like being exposed as an ignoramus. It was discouraging when he held to his puerile exposition of the thing in dispute. Useless to hope for analysis from Noel, yet Geraldine went on hoping that Noel would mature: in his choice of friends, his reactions to external events, his loving. But Noel made no choices, everyone had access; he was a receptacle for the stale ideas of others. Did this mean she'd wasted ten years of her life? Geraldine's heart couldn't accept it.

He was so sure of her, going back to her house as though it were his. Giving up but still hanging on.

It might have been two days or two weeks later that they left Cairns. Geraldine, sunk in a deep malaise, saw doves and middle-aged people in shorts and varicose veins. She was aware of the sea and the voices, sullen or smooth and treacherous. Storm clouds that hung all day on the horizon. Sometimes a shout of laughter from Don. Bernard squashing some toads before they left.

Tropical paradise scenery. Bluer blues, greener greens, colours so vivid they hurt. Island-dotted sea within the reef, green, sapphire, turquoise road along the edge through sugar. Hilly to the left. A sign said 'Trinity Beach, Captain Cook sailed these waters 1770 something-something'. A truck with a stack of cane slowed them up. Thirteen rivers to cross, Don said. One more river, and that's the river of Jordan. Spectacular pointy black hills ahead. They took the Mount Molloy turn-off, turning back sharp left. Thick red dust. Over the bloody axles, Don said. The Gorge and Devil's Thumb. Noel missing it all, he'd turned back. Big unfamiliar trees full of blossom. Piddling in the dust. Then sharp right again, onwards to the point. Difficult driving, a slow progress; nothing but dust. Don was as silent as she, Don too seemed to be brooding. They saw two taxis. The country got a bit flatter.

Late afternoon Don turned off the road into bush. It was a desolate place. Nearby was a derelict car; Geraldine had seen several. They made her remember death. A desolate place.

'I've had it,' Don said, getting out.

No sign of Bernard and Julie. Don began thrashing about with an axe, flattening scrub. Then he started on their tents. Geraldine watched without comment, lending a hand when he asked her to. Bernard's Land-Rover got in nearly an hour later. Bernard and Julie got out.

'Some bloody dump,' Bernard said exclusively to Julie.

'What the hell happened to you?' Don glared.

Bernard smiled at Julie and whispered something.

Julie came over to Geraldine. 'Tired?' she asked.

'No.'

Julie found no reply to that. For a moment she watched the men, pitching camp in record time as they burst with expletives and rancour, then said, 'People are all different, there's bound to be friction.'

Geraldine yawned. She knew disruptions couldn't happen among reasonable people, but there was no point in telling Julie this because Julie wouldn't comprehend. People made excuses. Trotted out differences in sex, background, way of life, interests, character, disposition. Noel made excuses for everyone, plucked them ready-made out of the air, for himself especially.

Geraldine helped Julie with the food. 'No city comforts up here,' Julie said.

Stirring the mess in the cauldron, eating her share along with the others. Bernard had arrived in a hat and still had it on, horribly floppy in soiled, white towelling.

'We had a flat,' Julie said.

'Why the hell couldn't you say straight off?' Don still had his anger.

'No damper again?' Geraldine smiled, watching the joke fall flat.

'No bushie eats damper if he can get bread,' Bernard said.

'Why'd we bring twenty kilos of flour then?' Don snarled.

'I wondered – '

'You said – '

'I said nothing; you were the know-all.'

Don turned his scowl from Bernard to Julie. Damper was a dirty word now.

'There are ways of doing things, why make it hard for yourself?' Did Bernard say that? Or Dennis in Sydney and a different context, months ago?

Voices reached her. The shouts went on. Geraldine's throat tightened and stayed as an ache.

Noel's weakness wasn't a revelation. Hadn't she always known and done her best to thrash it out with him? Noel vacillated because he couldn't face up, couldn't face truth, and people, and effort. He'd been the same with his job, giving it up. But this was worst of all – *he* was the one who'd been so keen. He'd asked her to go back too only because he was so sure she'd stick it out. How sly he'd looked, shifting from foot to foot in his moral flimsiness. He knew that being the person she was she'd go on alone to the end. He knew she was alone, the others not counting, that alone was being without Noel. He'd wanted a change from Noel's Den and even his precious Dennis could go by the board. Now it was Geraldine's turn for the lurch. He'd lumbered her with the others, no explanation, no consideration, just that he'd had enough, the fussing and jealousy jibes just facile excuses. *Qui s'excuse s'accuse*. She'd come along solely for his sake and Noel had pulled the mat out. He'd like to see her motiveless and stranded, but Geraldine never caved in, and Noel knew it. So he'd capitalised on it, hadn't he? Noel was tricky, sliding out of things. Even marriage. Perhaps his first wife was as blameless as Geraldine.

A plastic plate was thrust at her. 'Tuck in,' Julie said, tucking in herself. The dried pears and apricots had weevils in them. Geraldine refused with a nice smile.

The shouting had stopped. Clouds had settled on the men's faces. Gloom lay over the camp. Bernard had the look of a sulky delinquent.

They went to bed in the thundery atmosphere. Geraldine listened to the groaning stretchers and lay still on hers. She smiled at the unreason that kept them awake. It was a still night and she thought she would hear the dew drop plop by plop. It may have been pods bursting. One trained one's bladder on a junket of this sort, and kept an eye on one's bowels.

They de-tented next morning around eight. The bush was full of noise.

'Bloody birds,' Bernard said.

'The bastard's mad,' Don muttered to Geraldine.

About 100 metres along the road a lovely river, the Laura, with lawn-like grass under trees.

'We could've camped there,' she told Don.

'That's life, the bugger,' Don said.

At a spot called Road Junction they turned left. The other branch went out to Cooktown on the coast. A store and a hotel. Big smooth stones by the roadside, round and earth-red, like beach balls. A one-lane bridge approached between high banks of bright red earth. The Great Divide always visible, themselves highish on its slopes. Sudden switches in earth colour, that would rise to envelop the following vehicles, red to white to black; then yellow. Its thick choking dust stirred up as they ploughed through.

'Just passed a ruddy taipan,' Don said, 'bugger's dead.'

A sign on a post said Eternity. Geraldine picking her nose as they all did with the dust baked hard in the nostrils. Iron telegraph poles because of bushfires.

At the pub in the little town of Laura a man with stained false teeth told Geraldine, 'You get used to them.' He was speaking of the Aborigines. His nose was swollen and purple with pores like craters, and he had a few rotten teeth at the bottom where Geraldine could see strands of saliva like stitches as he spoke with his big loose mouth.

Geraldine took her beer outside. How they'd laugh back in the city. Aboriginal children laughed at her, their big dark eyes full of sorrow above big white grins. Geraldine smiled and got out her small loose change. Bernard took pictures of them.

Don got more whisky and Julie provisions. The Shell man told Don about the derelict cars. Some were ill-gotten on dishonoured HP agreements and abandoned when they broke down. Others were second-hand bombs not worth retrieving. Some were stolen. Passing motorists stripped them of parts until they were husks, left to rot and rust. Geraldine was strangely satisfied by the story of the derelict cars.

CHAPTER 8

And so it went on. Frayed tempers, ill-judged campsites. Ants got into the sugar, and the sugar bust into Julie's meat. Heat, humidity, mosquitoes. Geraldine lay at night in her instant canvas house digesting a dodgy dinner and was glad of her equilibrium as the others grew uncontrolled. The calmest person she knew. Geraldine at night longing for Noel inside the crazy orange. Poor Noel, he'd gone to pieces too. Geraldine looked through the little net square at shapes and shadows and tried to stop the whirl of impressions tumbling over each other: anthills like foreshortened elephants or maybe a group of Druids or huddle of sheep, and some like tombstones and some like Gothic cathedrals. A dirty river they'd paddled their hot feet in. Hot showers at a petrol depot. Three youths on motor bikes with sloganed sweat shirts. White, pink, yellow earth. Pettiness over meals.

Geraldine lay in the big still night and cursed the impulse that led her, Geraldine Whatsaname (rejecting even his name), to join this poisonous expedition she had to see through to its end. Noel's friends had expressed envy: I wish it was me, they said. Nothing like that ever happens to me. The hollow ring of their lies.

Noel had planned it all, lined up these people and established this elaborate journey just to be rid of her, knowing her strength, knowing she'd keep on when he turned back, saying those cruel untrue things deliberately. He hadn't given up, he'd never intended to go to the end. Noel had got her to come, all the time knowing he'd be returning at a pre-planned point. Perhaps she'd guessed all along and had made a challenge to herself. Noel was a drifter, taking the easy way out with smiling specious excuses.

Geraldine didn't like rough going but had a powerful will. Noel said she was perverse and headstrong, making his own sort of capital out of her fortitude. He knew she'd raise doubts, see ahead to the dirt and heat, and the lacks, and accidents and wrangles with improbable people they didn't even know. He knew she'd bypass these to be with him. So he'd enthused to get her going. Yet Geraldine supposed, as her tired eyes watched the light and shadow change through the little net window, there had to be some journey, a progress of one kind or another, a test of Noel. And everyone said what an opportunity, urging her to do something they'd never dream of doing themselves. The people they knew were the cheap, the *louche*, Noel's indiscriminate pick. But they'd been unwittingly right, because there had to be some end for a new beginning. Some point to reach. There'd been signs along the ten-year way, and Geraldine had shut her eyes to them, all the time feeling the inner sickening lurch towards emptiness, towards nothing. Like the Hawkesbury evening, the rush of love she'd felt, the yearning, her heart open and bleeding, then Noel's vulgar pun, a portent of the betrayal he planned hundreds of kilometres ahead.

Night after night longing for him. Her love for him the groove she was in.

Morning's black moods – the loud, pointless arguments, coarse voices, and sordidness. Where was the initial order Don had insisted upon? The childish holding of unspecified grudges. Julie too, all three nagging and drinking whisky, turned in on themselves, blind to the terrain. Bernard's unbridled clichés, his dirty floppy hat, his camera that was the cause of so many rows. The smell of them. All the build-up to the final explosion. Panic and emptiness.

At Musgrave a big timber house on stilts. A river. An airstrip. Birds in cages, a golden pheasant. Horses, Land-Rovers. A tree. It was a small tree and seen from a distance seemed covered with dusty grey foliage and pinkish blossoms. As their noise drew near the tree shook and broke into shouting cries and became a flight of birds. Galahs, pink and grey. Only bare branches and twigs remained, and the trunk. Noel would love it, but Noel was far away. Noel had given up at some place beginning with 'B'.

'Bloody galahs,' Don said.

Then a road of snow-white sand as fine as headache powders. Curving soon, winding through a weird sort of petrified forest, thin trees out of a low jungly growth with giant thick grey anthills dominating. Monuments. Shrines to a dead love. Dwarf palms with feathery tops and bulbous trunks, their hard bark looking like wrinkled stockings. Driving on into the night, Don nursing all his grudges. Bernard and Julie close behind with theirs.

They stopped eerily in a big bare circle among trees full of flying foxes. Don shot one for the fun of it. Incredible webbed wing structure, a dear little dead face. Brown hard gravelly ground. A circle in the bush, perhaps for flying saucers. No tents, stretchers under stars. Bernard backing so carelessly he shatters the rear window of his hired Rover. Fine starting-point for tantrums. That had to end somewhere.

CHAPTER 9

___

A rush of centuries, an aeon clicking by in swift images. A daze
of noise, silence, shouting. The depression was deep, and
Geraldine panicked against the rigidity and torpor that held
her. She clung to details, moment by moment, tiny shocks of
laughter or pain. It was only at night in the orange tent or
exposed to the stars that Noel flowed in with the big drawn-
out pain, or when she went deaf to the voices of the others. By
such measures she could cope for as long as she must.

There was no reason to note some things over others, but
was there reason in anything? Julie's sprained wrist.
Somewhere a nice cattleman in a blue check shirt, kindly and
talkative – was it at Coen where she replenished her tissues?
Filthy tea towels. A stink from among the provisions.

'You pull your weight or I'll bash your bloody head in.'
Don.

Bernard. 'That'll be the day.'

Welcome to Coen, it said. Mangoes and Bougainvillaea.
Little pointy mountains all about. Tin buildings, verandahs
with tree-trunk posts. Drink at John Harris Exchange Hotel,
topped by a black iron cut-out bugler on a prancing horse.
Julie in the butcher's. Look for cuscuses, someone said, a cross
between koalas and possums.

But sleeping every night when thinking ended.

'How to start a war by really trying – you've been swotting
it up, mate,' Don said.

A tumbling river among spotted rocks, the Archer. Total immersion. Washing day. A raging torrent, Don said they said, in the summer wet, 150 yards wide. To hell with bloody metrics, Don said. (This was winter, this sticky, enervating heat.) Big bloody boulders, look at 'em, Don said, chucked all over the scenery.

Flies, blowflies, ants, midges, mossies. And the continuing anthills. The road grey dirt, yellow sand, red earth, white sand. Don's pink-striped shirt, a penchant for pink. The still bush, palms, the eternal gums. Perpendicular dips to dry creek-beds. And sometimes rivers, flowing or not. Not a road, just a track. Don hacking branches for patches of erosion.

'A bloke could fall right in,' he said.

A million roots patterned in lattice across the eroded bits. It would all soon break up into nothing.

A fleeting stomach-ache. Julie awake with the pain in her wrist, poor thing.

Sydney was such a little place in this perspective, and Noel the merest dot alone in her house, missing her, poor darling. Dear Noel, deprived of all he took for granted: the things she did for him. Words were nothing. They flew away with all their cruelty. Love remained, not uprootable by crass words. At the Archer River camp she saw the immensity of sky, the innumerable stars, and moving across the vastness three silly man-made satellites, hugging earth, puny, ephemeral; eclipsed while eternity hung there. Then sleep, her nerves already braced for the morning shouts and grunts of these alien people Noel had thrown her among.

'Come and get it.' Don's coarse voice. But worse was Bernard's illiterate refinement.

Inertia. The smallest job an effort sapping energy. All of them.

They didn't use deodorants. Bernard's sulky resentful face all the time watching when Geraldine sought privacy with her toiletries and plastic bowl of water. Cowardly inaudible muttering. But once when she returned too soon she heard him say to Julie, 'She's up the bloody wall.' Then putting on an insolent face at the sight of her.

Slippery clay. Bumps, holes, stones. A constant jolting. Shut in the bush, so still, so hot, so antique. Millenniums gone in moments. Tell Noel the bush mystique is being dirty, laugh with him.

Big yellow single flowers on bare thin trees. Wild cotton, Don said.

A stagnant river of malodorous, slithery things. Overnight camp there. High steep banks, red mud, black brackish water in the dark where things hovered on slow big wings.

'Jesus, get stuck into something else and leave my camera alone.'

'Your bloody literature's great,' Don said with a laugh, 'Is that the talk they learn you in government offices?'

'Just take your paws off my camera, that's all.'

'Bloody cretin.'

They didn't bother with tents. Stretchers beside the slough of despond. Don guarding the last of the Scotch.

The man in the blue check shirt said, 'You take this present government.' Geraldine wasn't interested in governments, just in her personal life, just to get through it without hard roads, without barrenness, or hills and gullies and ensnaring roots. But Joe was a nice man, manager of a big cattle station. 'They run cattle,' he said, 'why should they spend money on roads and improvements? The politicians and bureaucrats don't care, it's all city problems and capital for them, and overseas money and tearing each other apart. Half this is owned by Yanks and the rest Poms, with the Japs looking for their slice. They don't give a shit so long as they stay in power. Me, I'm all right with all mod cons but the ordinary folk hereabouts get the wrong end of the stick, kerosene lamps and tank water storage and bugger you, Jack, I'm all right.'

She'd tell Noel about Joe, he'd enjoy it.

The Kennedy Road, a track barely discernible, losing it,

backtracking, wheel ruts in sandy jungle. Big white single flowers. Impossible creek crossings.

'Where's the bloody winch?

Poor young Edmund Kennedy, blazing a trail on horse-back and on foot.

The endless anthills ended. Up and over. Thick steamy rain forests shut in vaporous rain. Deep mysterious river, a curtain of lianes, enormous banana palms, twisted trunks of giant trees, the palpitation of life. They were axle-deep in wild flowers. Then down to a place on the coast called Portland Roads. A long jetty, small white beaches between mangroves. Two Belgians in a schooner round the world. A wharf for the weekly boat to Thursday Island, piles of timber and petrol drums, the old damp sea breeze.

Back again up the road to camp in a clearing. Giant ants and rusty petrol drums. Bernard inflicted a deep long scratch on the side of his hired Rover.

'Had a feeling you'd turn out a pest,' Don said.

'Took no risk then, did you?'

Life on the coral strand. Don got drunk that night.

Next day they cut their way with axe and saw. Blazing the overgrown trail, shifting fallen trees. Smell of the dank under-growth under the rotting leaves. Year after year after year. Over every crest the near-sheer drop to the next creek bed. Humid wind from the sea made soft glue on their bodies in the strong sun. Passing trees rat-tatted on the Rovers' sides. The peaks all left behind. Onwards to the unseen point. It took seven hours to do 27 kilometres.

The Pascoe River in the jungly hushed dusk. Overpowering stench of rotting. Crocodile skeleton. Bernard took its teeth.

Julie's stew used up a lot of odd cans.

'Bloody terrible,' Don said between great mouthfuls.

'What d'you expect, filet mignon?' Bernard said with an arch smile at Geraldine.

'Shut your trap,' Don said.

Then Bernard.

Then Don.

Loud, louder. Geraldine shut her ears. She'd cut her nails tomorrow. Tell Noel about Edmund Kennedy and civilisation. Noel was very close as the shouting got worse.

Then a different voice, Julie's. 'Well, that's it, I've had it, this is the end. I'm getting the nearest plane back. Talk about women! You blokes'd be hard to beat. Ask Gerry.'

Nobody did. More shouts. Crashes and jangles. A slap. A thud.

Don's voice thick with rage. 'Shoulda known you'd let me down.'

And Bernard. 'Who's bloody let who down!'

'All right, that's it, we've had it.'

'Get screwed.'

Geraldine said an unheeded goodnight and went into her tent. Tonight the tents were well spaced. She washed all the crucial bits carefully and lay down on her stretcher, smelling nice. Edmund Kennedy and the way life was here today: no supermarkets, not even a corner shop. Here they like silence and solitude (called loneliness by city folk) and feel sorry for us with our tensions and traffic fumes and bad news every day. Time not a clock-watching rush. Day follows night and night ends day. Time's a truck with seven months' supplies, or it's a two-month cattle muster, or a weekly boat with essentials. Or a butterfly breaking out of its chrysalis. There'd been some point to make – something significant to make Noel see. Never mind, it would come back.

She woke early and got up at once. How peaceful it was. Nothing moved, the sea thin glass beyond the mangroves. Geraldine unfolded a canvas stool to sit on and cut her nails. Kept short they didn't break. Then she brushed her hair. She could never let herself go like Julie. The flies were about already. She watched two crawl in single file up the right leg of her shorts. Best to keep covered, except somehow this morning it didn't matter. Picking her way with care she went for a stroll over deep thick spongy grass towards the mangroves. Everything was as still as the grave, the mangroves like make-believe scenery. She started through them. At once she was smothered in a cloud of dust that turned into minuscule life in blind attack. She fought her way out, dreading that her frenzy had been observed. There was nowhere to go except back to camp. The two men were up, ignoring each other. Don packing, slinging stuff about in a rage. Bernard gloomily smoking. Each intent on his own anger. There'd be no breakfast. Geraldine was glad, eager to start back.

She'd planned it to come from them and it had. She'd had to outlast them and had. This was their end. They didn't care about reaching Cape York, less than 200 kilometres ahead. No point for them in anything.

It was different for Geraldine. After Noel dropped out the point had been to hang on. Noel spoke of her turns and fits, but he was the one who flounced off. The dear silly, forgetting how he'd miss her. She felt like a conqueror whose foe is for ever subjugated. The way was clear now, and there was nothing to do but speed back to Noel.

Surprise him, the darling.

Part two

———

Five months later with Christmas almost on top of them the trip seemed buried with all past things. Noel had killed it off in her first week back.

But he couldn't wipe out Geraldine's memory and was unconcerned about the things that fed it. Even the weather: the southern summer so like the northern winter, the humidity seeming tinged with orange, and all the old problems the trip was meant to expunge intensified.

Her homecoming. The innocent surprise she'd planned. In the taxi from the airport, in the dark with lights and old city smells, her joy was nearly delirious. Because after all there was no place better for peacemaking than on their home ground. In her house.

It was all lit up as if in welcome. She hurried through the warm patio, past loud pushy people with drinks and laughter, into the living-room on such a high that the smooth young insolent girls there didn't matter. She couldn't see him. People stared. Strangers. It was Dennis who grabbed her, his brown eyes warm and welcoming.

'Well, well, the intrepid explorer, lovely to see you.' His eyes level with hers.

She was too tense for pleasantries. Somehow there'd been this picture of Noel alone, lonely, waiting.

Then Clyde, drunk, his arms round her and a wet sloppy kiss. And Jill Monro, small and slim and happy and smooth dark hair. And strangers staring. And Walter Hudson who was something small in oil in his fifties. Strangers staring at her boots and dirty pants and sweater. Then suddenly Noel, blank-faced, got by Dennis. A mite dishevelled.

'Goddess! Why didn't you wire or something?' And just too late his hug and a kiss that glanced off her cheek.

Geraldine threw herself at him. Let them all see. He was hers, this house hers. She clung to him and buried her face against him and felt his arms go round her. If they had any sensitivity they'd go. Why didn't they go? The time-eaters snatching her joy, crowding her in, crowding her out. Not even a Sunday; Thursday, to be exact. No fervent pressure in Noel's arms that were round her simply in reflex.

She pulled her face away and looked up at him. It was nice that she had to look up at Noel. 'My stuff's in the drive, darling, would you? I'll just streak up for a shower and be back and join in the fun. Hope there's some food, I'm famished.'

'Tons of grub. I'll stow your gear in the carport. And Geraldine?'

She turned her smiling face.

'Welcome home,' Noel said grinning.

'Thank you, darling.' Geraldine ran upstairs. In a feverish rush telling herself don't worry, it was just Noel's funny way of being lonely. Things would change now she was back.

Half an hour later she was downstairs again. Healthy, out-doorsy and capable over the secret vulnerability. Men's eyes fastened on her breasts, but that was all the notice taken of her. It looked that sort of party, casual and fleshy. Her homecoming.

She found Noel in the kitchen. About ten people, careless food, a mess all over her precision.

'Darling, what lovely smells, did you do it all?' Back in the old tense carefree role.

'Had a hand,' Noel said, and after a brief glance added, 'Don't you look nice.'

Two people were helping Noel. A fair silent man nearly as tall as Noel. A supple short girl with a faint proprietary smile and smooth brown skin, too much of it exposed. A lot of dis-organisation. Deafening noise, shouts of laughter and a glass splintering, and between each burst the sustained blowfly buzz from the living-room.

'Know everyone, angel?' Noel said as he dived again at the oven.

Andrew saluted with a finger and Gail in one of her hand-woven sacks blundered towards Geraldine with a big happy smile. Geraldine watched Noel peep at a steaming dark mess in her expensive imported casserole. There was hot garlic bread, too, and numerous hot and cold side things. She felt Gail pull at her hand.

Noel said, 'That's Frank Clifford at the end there, Eliot Cross in the purple velvet – Jesus, is it still women and children first? Sorry about that – Dawn and Rita, Susan over there, Brian behind her – '

Geraldine wanted to scream that it didn't matter.

'Jim Oates my right-hand man and Nerida Jessop my left. I've left some out but who cares?'

Geraldine had pushed her way through to him, with Gail still hanging on. 'Want any help?' she asked in a bright voice. Why is Eliot Cross? ran in the dark of her mind.

'No thanks, goddess, it's all in hand. Matter of fact, you can all clear out so we can get the bloody stuff organised and distributed.' He must mean the others, not her. 'On wheels,' he added with a silly smile. He was swaying a bit.

Geraldine opened a drawer and got out a chef's apron. She got behind Noel and placed the halter over his head, then with her arms round him straighted the rest of it and started tying the strings.

'For Chris'sake,' Noel said, 'what's going on?' He jerked his head round. 'Jesus, I might have known,' he muttered.

There was a low liquid gurgle to her left. Geraldine's eyes met the amused ones of the short supple girl who was Noel's left-hand man. Nerida Something. Shapely limbs sticking close to Noel. The laugh taunting Geraldine.

Gail pulled her away. 'Come and tell me about your trip, I'm dying to hear all about it.' Kindly, cow-like Gail steering her out of her own kitchen in a relentless sort of way. Well, why not? Geraldine felt suddenly listless. She let Gail find them a place in a corner, Geraldine in an arm-chair and Gail on a floor cushion at her feet.

'Now then?' Gail said.

So Geraldine told her the things Gail wanted to hear, mechanically ran over terrain and weather and distance, the dead taipan, one live kangaroo, the galahs, flying foxes, all the birds in the teeming loneliness. The anthills. She had to shout.

Gail looked plumper. 'Did you see any bush turkeys?' she asked.

'Tons,' Geraldine lied. 'You pregnant?'

'Yes,' Gail said, actually blushing. Gail had two children and wanted lots more and everyone knew she lived with Andrew only so she had the means at hand. She thought men silly but natural, unlike artificial insemination. Gail liked everything natural: food, clothing, childbirth. She made plastic things at home to help stamp out leather. She had horrid long straight hair full of natural dandruff. She encouraged Andrew in his sculpting.

Geraldine answered her questions without thought, her mind on all these noisy people, some old and a lot new, and how to get rid of them. The food was making its appearance and with it Noel's right-hand and left-hand men. Gail followed her eyes.

'Pretty, isn't she? Doesn't give a damn about anything, or so they say.'

Just then Claire Sayers sidled towards Geraldine. Shy and conformist, supposed to be Dennis's fiancee. The story he put about. Short fluffy red hair and pale blue eyes.

'Nice to see you back, Geraldine.'

'Thanks, nice to *be* back. How's everything going?'

Claire knew she meant Noel's Den. 'A huge success, they're being featured in a series of wine commercials just now.'

'Splendid,' Geraldine shouted.

More people collected round her. Geraldine let Gail, who was crazy about birds and beasts and flowers and trees, do most of the talking for her. Her eyes found Noel, alone with Nerida. Someone thrust a plate of food and a paper napkin at Geraldine. She took both, then in a few moments put them aside. It was only twenty past ten. She thought Noel caught her eye but he pretended not to, bent even closer to the girl, who didn't give a damn.

'You must be terribly tired,' Gail said suddenly, with a searching look at Geraldine's face.

'It's all been pretty non-stop,' Geraldine said, and just then realised that no one had said anything about Noel's return weeks earlier, about five weeks. That meant there'd been one of his easy lies.

Nerida was dancing now, alone, everyone watching. Snaky, wiggly, overtly sexy. Noel attempted to join in, but Nerida evaded him in a teasing manner that somehow, Geraldine thought, made him part of it. It became a chase. People seemed to find it uproariously funny. As if it were something familiar, some act they had enjoyed again and again. Dennis came and sat by her. Or perhaps by Claire.

A few people were drifting off, calling careless goodbyes, the Hudsons among them. The Monroes came over specially to say goodnight to Geraldine; they had a recent baby and sitter problems. Dennis was talking about the Den's prosperity and popularity. The tall quiet fair man was down on his haunches at Geraldine's right. She was vaguely aware of him because he too seemed to be watching Noel and Nerida.

Then Nerida clapped her hands to get attention. Noel's slow sexy smile was on her. 'Anyone want more food?' Nerida asked. 'There's piles left.'

No one took up the offer.

'It's sheer waste,' Nerida declaimed, 'all those starving millions everywhere, famine all over the place, crop failures, the oil crisis, droughts – '

'We solve it by overeating?' some man broke in wittily.

'Oh, you make me sick,' Nerida said with anger Geraldine thought simulated. The cheek of it – *her* food in *her* house.

'It's a great little social conscience.' Noel grabbed Nerida by the scruff of her neck. 'Come to the kitchen, wench, and eat it yourself.' And with that excuse he got her to himself; with that little bit of by-play they got away together.

She could feel the fair man's eyes. Geraldine got up suddenly, causing the whole group round her to break up. She was restless for it to be over.

'God, you must be tired,' Dennis said, but his warm brown eyes didn't fool her; he meant she showed every haggard year of her age. 'Bad night for Noel's first party,' he added.

Geraldine knew he was lying but couldn't be bothered. Without ceremony she started shooing them out and very soon everyone got the message. She found Noel beside her in the patio and saw Nerida leaving among the crowd.

When they were all seen safely off Noel came back in and said at once, 'Sorry, angel, about the party, you should've let me know.'

He didn't *see*. 'It's all right,' Geraldine said smiling.

'No, really,' Noel said, 'I could kick myself. What a night to choose for the first nosh-up.'

Oh, really? The same lie as Dennis, but of course. 'What about the clearing-up?' Geraldine said, fighting against depression.

'Not you, that's for sure. I've got Mrs Mac lined up for the morning but right now off you go upstairs while I whip round the ashtrays and stuff.'

Geraldine went upstairs. He did seem genuinely sorry, but the sounds of remorse are easy. She sat at the dressing-table and listened to the thumps and thuds and a crash or two from downstairs.

When he came up she turned with a smile. 'Claire told me about the wine ads.'

'Yes, good show, isn't it?' he dragged his sweater off.

'Being in the know, so to speak.'

'And business is good.'

'Blooming.'

She stood up swiftly. 'Oh darling, it's nice to be back.'

'That's a nice dress,' Noel said and went into the bathroom. Dodging her with a compliment. The dress in fine black wool was a favourite of Noel's, long and clinging to reveal her fine body lines, long sleeves and a square neck. Tomorrow she'd give it to Mrs Mac or chuck it in the Smith Family bag.

Noel came back in his dressing-gown. Neither mentioned their last scene together. Geraldine was naked under her open robe.

'I've got so much to tell you,' she started impulsively. 'You missed all the best part.' Noel was yawning on the side of his bed with dropping eyelids. 'It's not really barren at all, it's only because – '

'Not tonight, angel, I'm a bit all in, d'you mind?'

The anthills were on the tip of her tongue, and Joe King the cattleman. Noel caught the look on her face.

'Tell you what,' he said, getting into bed, 'I'll come home for dinner tomorrow, Dennis won't mind, and you can tell me all about it then.'

Big deal.

Just the same she got into his bed after her shower. She had to wake him. They made love but Noel seemed far away. Afterwards she tried to talk, talking to emptiness. It was so clear in her head, how the anthills and the others' split-up and Joe's exposition of conditions in the Peninsula and Edmund Kennedy, how every plant and bird and mile covered all led to the conclusion, the knowing, the point: they were made for each other. His mouth was open and a dribble came out one side.

Why is Eliot Cross? Downsliding towards despair and Eliot Cross and the small shapely girl and the point of the trip slipping out of her grasp.

Noel was home next day at seven-thirty. He'd said seven, but the crazy traffic, he said.

Geraldine and Mrs Mac had been four hours cleaning up, only a quarter-hour coffee break. Mrs Mac was delighted that Geraldine was back. She couldn't say who'd missed Geraldine more, Mr Blaine or herself. She said Mr Blaine had been a lot quieter since he came back. She said he'd changed a lot.

'No parties?' Geraldine smiled.

'Not a one till last night, dear.'

So it was true. Mrs McIntyre didn't lie. Couldn't be bothered, she said; with her bad memory she'd land in the soup lying. Mrs McIntyre was a deserted wife in her late forties. She came on Fridays and Tuesdays to clean and at any other time she was required. She didn't think it was right for Geraldine to do dusting and cooking and washing, machines or no, but Geraldine liked to. She paid Mrs McIntyre well, knowing her worth. Mrs McIntyre wore a rigid claret-coloured bouffant hairdo which she had recharged every Thursday. Her natural colour was mouse, she said disparagingly. 'You just miss mouse,' she told Geraldine. 'Honey's more what you are.' She liked Geraldine more than she liked Noel, but that went for all men, who down the centuries and *en masse* had made sure women got the wrong end of the stick. Noel teased her, flinging his arms round her and professing unabated and unrequited passion, and Mrs Mac said, 'Now, don't you come the raw prawn, Mr Blaine.'

At dinner, a special effort of shortcrust steak and kidney pie, one of Noel's favourites (or it used to be), having him trapped with his mouth full, Geraldine got the Peninsula stuff off her chest. She told him about Joe King, the station manager in the blue check shirt.

'Appearances are deceptive, darling. It's only barren because the rivers flow away to the gulf. There's plenty of water in the wet season, too much, floods. It's just not being harnessed, Joe said, so after drowning cattle and crops it runs away without being put to use. The land only looks parched, Joe said, but really it's alive because it adapts to its conditions.'

As I must, she thought, watching Noel's abstraction.

'Nice pie, darling?'

'Jolly good,' Noel said, 'we had it as yesterday's dish.'

'Nice as this?'

'Well,' he looked at her, 'perhaps yours has the edge.'

'Joe said the people who live up there feel cut off from main events. They're thinly scattered and without the numbers to force constructive change. And he said being alien there they haven't the adaptive skill of the Aborigines or of birds, plants and animals.'

She paused. Noel was pushing his beans around.

'Joe said that after billy tea, tea in a teapot is the end. There was a lot more, darling; he was terribly interesting and said it was a treat talking to me.'

Noel grinned, then laughed. 'Seems to me Joe was looking for a good instant lay.' And reached for the wine.

The short supple girl jumped into her mind, Nerida Something. 'How long've you known her, darling?'

'Who?'

'Whatever her name is, the girl last night you were dancing with.'

'You're not going to start making mountains.'

'A simple straightforward question.'

'Hum.'

'You didn't say how long?'

'Jesus, I dunno, a few months more or less.'

Since before the trip. The journey might never have been, it was all for nothing. Worse. She yearned to communicate with Noel. She would never adapt to his loss of interest.

'Tomorrow's Saturday, darling, couldn't you have it off?

'Not a hope, angel, it's one of our busiest days.' He lit a cigarette, forgetting how she hated it at the table. Or perhaps not forgetting.

'I was thinking, Noel, why not employ someone, even two extra, if you're doing as well as everyone says. I'm sure Dennis would be all for it.'

'He lives for the place, loves every minute.'

'You, then – you look so tired, darling.'

Instead of replying directly Noel turned sideways with his glass and cigarette and stared across at the Stubbs horse on the dark red wallpaper. Then he said, 'It's a tiring old world.'

'Salad, darling?'

Noel shook his head.

'Cheese? It's only mousetrap but when I get time – '

'No thanks, goddess, nothing else.' Except of course wine, of course, and of course he was going to finish the bottle and perhaps another.

She'd meant to tell him about Edmund Kennedy, but the point of it still eluded her. It was barren ground in any case. Noel wouldn't know Edmund Kennedy from a bar of soap, most likely would crack his stale coarse instant lay joke again.

Geraldine put music on while they had their coffee to stop herself questioning him. Cherish the frail union, then gradually build it up. She tried not to look at him because his head was full of Nerida Something. When the record was finished, she got him to tell her about the advertising campaign for wine built around Noel's Den. Noel came alive then. A long dreary boring tale without any point, bewildering, extraneous, featuring a stunning model called Rachel.

'How did you get back?' she asked.

Noel looked blank.

'From wherever it was you left us?'

'Oh, Bowen. Went on to Townsville and got a plane.'

'I see.'

Noel went to bed while Geraldine washed up. He pretended sleep when she got gently into his bed. She nibbled his cheek and ear and whispered, 'What made Eliot Cross?'

'Mm? Oh, I see.' A condescending smile with shut eyes. 'I'm trying to give it up.'

'Good, it's so childish.'

'So I'm told.'

———

A party somewhere. The Christmas season with its mandatory gaiety forced the realisation that Noel had cut the ground from under her feet: party-wise Geraldine hadn't a leg to stand on. Noel's friends no longer had the run of her house. He'd demolished that area of complaint. The troubling thing now was the absence of parties. And Noel's own absence. On Sundays too, often far into the night, and so evasive when Geraldine remonstrated that his presence became a worse emptiness. The insistent awareness of Nerida compounded the torment. There was no proof, just certainty. She'd seen Nerida only a couple of times, once when a Sunday carload picked Noel up, another time when the weather was warming and they came back early for a dip in her pool, about six of them. Geraldine didn't join in, just watched from the edge of a window with aching eyes.

The new worry was five months old, a lifetime. The determined high Geraldine had returned on in July had swung to the depths. The house echoed with emptiness. Yet Geraldine had the impression of non-stop merriment going on beyond her reach. In her loneliness she looked forward to Tuesdays and Fridays when Mrs McIntyre came, and manufactured reasons for her to come more often. At first she invited women for lunch or tea in the hope their gossip might entwine Noel with Nerida. She wanted confirmation of her misery. Yet they seemed to know nothing, and their visits depressed her. Their talk bored her. They said nothing to substantiate the torment. They were the wrong women, anyway. The women Geraldine could tolerate refused to acknowledge the Neridas of the world: embodiment of the permissive, promiscuous, free-and-easy society they hoped God would one day smite.

The only one to mention Noel was old sobersides Faye Hudson, Walter's wife, and in a complimentary way. They'd noticed, she and Walter, a marked improvement in Noel after his trip up the coast; a sobering, a new attitude of responsibility. He'd grown out of parties, Noel told Walter, thus pleasing both Hudsons. Faye's daughter Lynette chimed in with the same. Lynette was a poisonous female of twenty-six still trying to make up her mind what to do, if anything, with her life. She'd flunked university and was waiting for Mister Right. In the meantime when she felt like it he annoyed her mother in Faye's flower shop. The Hudson women knew how glad Geraldine must be at the change in Noel because, despite her staunch behaviour, they'd always known she was a fish out of water at his parties.

This thing today was the first of the Christmas lot. The same old blur, the familiar loud false cries of undying friendship, the usual people with the usual names. The people Noel knew were interchangeable: this week's Angela, Michael and Dorothy might next week turn into Margaret, John and Sandra; to Geraldine they were the same people combining to ruin her marriage and her life. It was all so exactly the same it was hard to believe some more profound change had taken place.

It was Sunday morning in somebody's garden, hours of drinking before lunch which would just be the same thing with platters of food thrown in. Geraldine was introduced by a man she didn't know to people she didn't want to know, Noeline Something, Polly, Somebody O'Donnell and a quiet man called Jim. At least he seemed quiet because he didn't scream at the joy of meeting her at last, didn't try to strangle her with a drunken hug. No face registered because Geraldine had eyes only for Nerida, and for Noel in Nerida's context.

Noel was four years older but such a child. Where was the sober responsibility he'd fooled the Hudsons with? Tipsy, lovable, naughty. They still made love sometimes, but even when Noel started it going he somehow eluded her; even when she held his body it wasn't Noel in her arms. His spirit was elsewhere, with Nerida. Geraldine had a robot in a widening, sickening void.

'We've already met,' a quiet voice said close to her ear, 'the night you came back from the trip.'

It was the fair man. As if she cared. Geraldine barely glanced at him. Why didn't the fool go away?

They still made love, she could never resist Noel. Nobody could. So Nerida couldn't resist him. If there'd been thousands of others it didn't matter. Only Nerida mattered. Geraldine felt a wave of faintness.

She pushed her way through people who moved indifferently, not even looking, the shove-and-grab people she hated. There were chairs about and benches. Geraldine found a garden chair tipped over. She righted it and sat down, shutting her eyes to shut out the lovebirds, alone together now, Noel's arm along the vine-covered wall as he bent intimately over the lovely silly face of Nerida Something. But even with tight-shut eyes she saw them.

She wasn't so lucky to have the darling now. They all saw it, they all knew. They pitied her. Noel's darlingness, never specified, was all showered upon Nerida for everyone to see. It was Nerida now who was lucky to have the darling. Geraldine still had the darling in her house, legally tied in marriage, but Nerida had all the luck.

A voice from somewhere down beside her. 'I'm planning a trip up there myself.' Through a maze of misery and rage Geraldine glanced at the fair man who was down on his haunches beside her, chewing a blade of grass, at ease, quiet, at peace. His very blue eyes met hers and then he looked across at Noel and Nerida. Geraldine sighed. She wished he'd go away. Why didn't he join in the fun? That's what parties were for.

'Like a drink?' the quiet voice asked.

'No, thank you.' I'm leaving almost immediately. Had she said that aloud? It didn't matter. Just remain negative and everything would go away. Watching the lovebirds, so right together.

'I've got a few kids interested. I've got some leave due and at that time of year, winter, I can wangle a bit extra. What I was wondering – I hoped – I mean having been once you'd know all the pitfalls, what to avoid, what to take, that sort of thing. If you could bear it again – sometimes you see far more the second time around.'

Was she dreaming? He must be mad. Jim Something, she remembered. She gave him a vacant look.

'I thought this coming year,' he said.

Geraldine scarcely heard him. The lovebirds had gone. Her eyes were everywhere. This wretched persistent insignificant man had got in the way of her watchfulness.

At that instant she was hugged from behind, two squeezing arms pressed round her breasts. Geraldine jerked forward. 'Don't touch me,' she ground out, and turned to the laugh in Noel's eyes.

'Only me, goddess, no ogres today. Come and have some grub before they eat it all.'

The fair man was on his feet, watching. She turned her back on him.

'Darling,' she said, 'sorry, the noise and heat.' She saw Dennis and Claire had joined them.

'Like to go?' Noel said.

'Oh, *yes*.'

'Stand a spot of lunch first, so they don't think we only came for the grog?'

'All right, darling.' Holding tight to his hand she turned a comically rueful smile on Dennis and Claire. 'He always gets his own way, doesn't he?' And got their obedient smiles.

The four of them pressed into the buffet crowd, Geraldine keeping her tight grip for as long as possible.

She didn't see Nerida again at that party. It explained Noel's attentiveness, but it was better than nothing. Was it too much to expect the thing was dying? In the light of Noel's fickleness and Nerida's free-and-easiness – scarcely the foundation for lasting love – it wasn't too much to expect, was it?

The fair man had gone too, with his ludicrous and irritating second-trip idea.

One down, three to go, Geraldine thought later under the shower. Four parties in one week would be an endurance test. It was around three-thirty now, and she looked forward to drinks by the pool, just the two of them quiet after a swim. She made herself take a whisky sometimes with Noel simply to be companionable, perhaps remove another cause for reproach. The occasions were rare enough in any case.

It was while she was brushing her hair that she heard the noise start. Car doors slamming, whoops and cries and laughter. For a moment she went rigid with anger, then suddenly limp as the bottom dropped out of the day. It was like groping through inert pitch-black to get from the bedroom to a spare one at the back where she could look down on the pool. Noel striding along its edge in shorts, hands outstretched to Nerida's hands, Nerida leading a small noisy bunch of revellers looking swim-clad.

Geraldine bit her knuckles to stop the tears. If she started she'd never stop. Because this was no surprise visit. Noel had invited them without telling her. She wouldn't accuse him because she didn't want his little-boy remorse, because she no longer trusted it. Didn't they ever get tired? Four hours of what they called fun had already exhausted her. Had it? Mentally, yes. Spirit and body were ready to cope and conquer.

Back in the bedroom Geraldine put on a one-piece white swimsuit and a short yellow towelling robe, then in bare feet ran downstairs. By the time she got to the pool her smile was stuck in place.

'Hi there, glad you could all come.'

Noel turned sharply. 'Thought you'd flaked out, goddess.'
She caught the momentary annoyance.

'Flaked out? *Me*?'

They all laughed and Clyde, swaying on the edge of the
pool at the portentous stage of drunkenness, said, 'Gerry's a
man at heart.'

'Well, of all the nerve! Chauvinist pig!' That was Elaine
Thorpe and on the last word she gave Clyde a shove that toppled him into the pool.

Dear God, the everlasting horseplay! The gaiety!
Geraldine curled up with her smile on the edge of the pool,
determined to outlast them, to watch, determined to prevent
any truancy of Noel with Nerida.

Clyde climbed out, spluttering, with a helping hand from
Kevin Monro. Kevin's wife Jill would be at home with the
baby. It wasn't a usual grouping. Clyde and Elaine, Kevin,
Nerida and the fair man who was Jim Something. Clyde and
Elaine didn't like each other, Geraldine knew, and tried to
hide their real animosity with a simulated dislike that was
meant to be lighthearted. Elaine Thorpe did commercial art-
work. In her fifties, caustic, short iron-grey hair and a light
moustache. She lived alone in a terrace house in Redfern.
Geraldine knew Elaine was tagged lesbian, but unnatural
practices were of as little interest to Geraldine as the natural
substances and processes that were Gail's hang-up. Like the
great big world Noel teased her with – what had Geraldine
to do with that? Kevin was twenty-nine, conventional, in a
bank. He'd met Jill there and they'd followed the old routine
of wooing, engagement, wedding and parenthood. Only
when Jill was tied up at home Kevin sometimes let his short
hair down.

Behind her wide all-embracing smile Geraldine watched
her target. Noel lying full-length on the opposite edge of the
pool, his face on his arms turned to Nerida, his eyes all over
her. Nerida flaunted his desire in every move, in the silly
smiles and coquettish hair tossings, in every wriggle and twist.

At that distance she looked like any glowing healthy young female. Geraldine wanted closer inspection. Suddenly Nerida laughed, jumped up and dived into the pool. A belly-smacker. Small and supple but no watersprite. But Noel's absorbed gaze was still unbearable. It wasn't Nerida's water record he was after. He was sitting now with his legs dangling over the side. Thirty-four; he'd never keep up with Nerida's pace; some comfort in that. He stood up and dived in; they were all in now. The fair man was monopolising Nerida so Noel had to bobble alone. The fair man was saying something, perhaps trying to get another recruit for his Peninsula trip. What a bore everything was.

Geraldine shot to her feet, stood poised for a moment, then made a perfect dive, feeling her body cut clean as a knife through the water. She rose almost at the other end of the pool, exhilarated by her own prowess and by all their watching eyes. She had the edge in this element and it never failed to win Noel's praise. Today it was just what she needed. Levering herself with her strong arms she got lightly out of the pool, shook her hair and wrapped herself in the yellow robe. Then suddenly Nerida followed her, taking much longer, puffing a bit. Close to Geraldine.

'You're fabulous,' Nerida said.

Geraldine smiled and nudged the big cushion with her foot and said, 'Sit here with me and watch the fun.'

Nerida's bikini was just about invisible. The body of a child, but Geraldine knew it wasn't. 'D'you do anything?' she asked in a kind voice, 'any job, any interests?'

Nerida shrugged. 'I'm secretary to a solicitor just now, but nothing's permanent, is it?'

'I don't know, isn't it?'

'Well, look, I mean the world – it's crazy to get hung up on anything – God!'

Geraldine smiled tolerantly. 'No plans like marriage or anything?' A neat little face, nothing more, shallow grey eyes.

'You're joking,' Nerida said, 'I mean – I don't mean *you*,

you're different – I mean kids like me, no thanks, not on your life.'

'It seems – unstable.'

'The whole scene's unstable,' Nerida said. 'It might all vanish overnight, the way I see it.'

A glowing golden skin, not a blemish. 'D'you live with your parents?' Geraldine's idle question masked the close study she made of the girl beside her: small even teeth, firm forceful brown eyebrows, fine shining hair that hung over her shoulders as it dried, the ready, world-weary, lascivious smile.

'Shit, no. Oh, sorry.' Childish hand over mouth. Geraldine shook her head, smiling it didn't matter. 'God, no, we didn't mix. I got out two years ago. *I* didn't make the work, *I* didn't ask to be born, did I?'

Sheeplike, one of the sheep, a sheep's instability. 'Seventeen?' Geraldine guessed.

'Nineteen. And a bit.'

'What about abroad?' Geraldine asked. 'Don't you want to travel?'

Nerida was a shrugger. She shrugged again. 'Some day, I guess – yes, I guess so, if it's all still there.'

Geraldine was sweet and kind and sympathetic, and lofty in her security as Noel's wife and head of all this domain, all the time aware of Noel watching from the pool where he pretended to disport with Elaine. Geraldine was having fun of her own in a heart-breaking sort of way.

'You're very pretty,' she said.

Nerida seemed not to hear because they were all heaving out of the pool now and towelling and shouting, and Noel went inside all wet for the bar-trolley, and there was ice clinking and a lot of talk about Noel's Den and the extension under way. This was the first Geraldine had heard of the extension.

'Is that where Noel met you?' she asked Nerida.

'Uh-huh.'

Geraldine hadn't been once to the Den since her return at the end of July, because somehow the Den epitomised the rot.

The two bits of news twisted together in her head: the Den was his home from home, and because he'd met Nerida there Noel was making it into a shrine.

'I'm serious, Mrs Blaine.' Geraldine turned her head to blue eyes.

'About the trip,' he added, 'your experience would be invaluable, and your maturity.' The fool really did mean it. He thought she'd enjoyed it the first time. He had a nice smile. She brushed him off once and for all. 'It's out of the question,' she said and she got up and moved away.

Noel kept them there for an outdoor barbecue. Only Kevin left because he'd promised Jill. There were millions of flying ants and beetles. It was after ten o'clock when the house died down.

Geraldine was in bed when Noel came up. She'd looked at herself in the glass and thought of Nerida, of Nerida's skin, of Noel kissing that skin goodnight, all over.

I was never like that, glowing like that.

It wasn't make-up. Nerida's shine came from inside, from something transcending youth.

Even at nineteen I was never like that.

Geraldine's skin looked dryish in the lamplight.

She didn't shower and wash her hair as she'd meant to. She knew when Noel was there because he said something, some trivial something that came from a great height and didn't reach down far enough for her to hear. She was in her own bed, turned facing the wall.

———

CHAPTER 12

Geraldine spent a lot of time at her pool. She was a strong swim-mer and would go its length a hundred times without tiring. In the first month of the new year it was automatic to put on a swimsuit after her shower, go downstairs when Noel had gone and get coffee and a piece of toast, then go straight to the pool. She didn't dive in at once. She waited until the little breakfast was safely on its way. She no longer worried about Noel's break-fast. Often she hated him first thing in the morning.

Even if it were raining she would still plunge into the pool, and afterwards, depending on the wind, sit on the canopied swing-seat beside the pool and stare at the lashed water, or else go in and mope about the house waiting for the rain to stop.

Mrs Mac now came every day. She was delighted when Geraldine suggested it just after Christmas. It meant more money and a filling-up of her time. 'Keeps me off the telly,' she said, sounding relieved. Mrs Mac did all the housekeeping. Without Mrs Mac the house would go to pot. It was only some deep and unexplored instinct that kept Geraldine from asking her to live in.

Geraldine had eight swimsuits, all one-piece: three black, three white, one acid yellow and one olive green. Always before diving, poised on the brink, she would admire the reflection in the water: the short hair, the firm curvy body with its study long legs and the powerful arms and shoulders.

She would compare it with another body, preferred over hers, and then she would plunge in and hear anger in the splash of water to match her own. In between swimming she'd lie on the edge never quite in the sun, away on a fantasy trip that sometimes took her to gleaming heights and often into a valley where all was dark; a lot of lonely time of confused thought; a sorting of priorities. Out of the desolate jumble in her head a few things emerged with clarity. The unimportant ones she would let drift off over the trees, Andrew and Gail, for instance. Andrew Lee, the quiet carpenter to whom she'd been so kind, Andrew who never popped around now as he'd used to. And kindly plump Gail Wallace who lived with Andrew and was so eager to be liked, yet not eager enough to pick up the phone or drop in to bubble over about the imminent baby. At the Christmas parties there'd been distrust in their eyes before they edged away. They'd gone sour, her friends who'd switched to Noel and were now part of Noel's conspiracy. They didn't matter and they blew off over the trees.

The blue transparent water as clear as her thoughts.

The same applied to the rest of the poisonous crowd. Only Dennis didn't fit into this category because Dennis was inherently part of Noel's Den.

Sometimes Geraldine forgot about lunch and Mrs McIntyre would call her in to it or bring something out on a tray. Nerida stayed with her at the pool, the evil chid's body in and out with her, clouding the water, spoiling Geraldine's summer, invading her solitude. Nerida who allowed Geraldine no peace. She wouldn't remember Nerida's surname, she knew it was Jessop but shut her mind to it. Nerida was a silly name, and Jessop as silly as Lemming.

She knew now Nerida was *it*. That thought stayed.

Her feeling for Noel changed as the day advanced. With the mellowing of afternoon she thought there might be something still to salvage. Was it useless to dream along these lines? Mightn't he be grateful to have the blinkers whipped from his eyes? Often she longed to be in his arms. Yet when he touched her she would jerk away. There were times when he gave her the hug of habit, and Geraldine would flinch and sometimes yell, 'Don't touch me,' because Noel caressing Nerida was all that she could see. Touch Nerida, she cried inside, Nerida's all you want.

And Nerida wanted Noel. Nerida was after more than Noel; she wanted Geraldine's house too, another thought that stayed.

Cruel, egotistical Noel, a thistledown, a cheap balloon whisking willy-nilly away from the piercing, deflating needle of her fine judgement. Geraldine sighed and stared at the blue water and wondered again if there was time for Noel to stop and listen before it was too late. He was her husband and this childish, headlong, pathetic infatuation reflected on the choice she'd made. All the bad, silly things about him – his convivial-ity, his awful funniness – had got a lot worse since Nerida. While it was true that Noel gagged his puns, he still got in a humorous dig about his vasectomy. Once during the Christmas blur, when great fat Gail said she'd like twenty babies, Noel said, 'In this house we're strictly ZPG, aren't we, angel?' And everyone laughed, knowing why he said it, remembering his puns. Noel's lack of taste was worse than theirs because he was her husband. Wasn't it a waste of time even to try to point this out to him? Long before Nerida her considerate attempts had met with no success. Babies of all things. Would he take them to Noel's Den every day and rear them with one hand while the other stirred today's dish?

Babies would drop from Nerida like rotten fruit from a neglected tree. Arrive without pain and flourish without effort. But it wasn't for babies that Noel was mad for her.

Noel wanted to supplant Geraldine with Nerida. A convic-tion that wouldn't go.

Sometimes Geraldine would still be there at sunset, still brooding down at the pool, not seeing the cottonball clouds turn from salmon to mauvey-grey and then to indigo against background streaks of yellow and palest green. If Mrs McIntyre cried a warning about evening chills, Geraldine would come to with a start and see only massive sunsets up in the Peninsula, aeons away in those wild and magnificent skies. These skies were drab, small and orderly as her resignation.

She knew Mrs Mac would come out to the pool and fidget about on its edge and urge Geraldine to go out somewhere, a picture show perhaps. Or throw herself into some activity that interested her. Or ring up one of her friends and go out somewhere nice like the zoo. Geraldine would smile and say she was fine.

One hot day at the start of February Geraldine paced the pool before her first plunge. Humidity lay in the air like lead. Geraldine had on her tightest white swimsuit. It was a very strange thing that worry had filled her out and her breathing felt constricted by the swimsuit. Slowly she went back in and upstairs, stripped off the white suit and put on her oldest black. Mrs Mac watched her come downstairs and go outside again and Geraldine knew the woman's face had a worried look. She plunged straight into the pool and under water she thought, How do they plan to do it? She came up and swam lazily around the pool. How was Noel going to effect the exchange? Geraldine climbed out, shook herself and sat staring at the water. She had no consoling habit or drug. She didn't smoke, she didn't bite her nails. She heard Mrs Mac come out.

'Why not dress up, dear, and go and give Mr Blaine a nice surprise at the Den?'

Go to Noel's Den. Why not? Geraldine smiled. 'I'll think about it.' The woman went back inside looking pleased.

Noel's Den was the obvious next move, maybe the last she would make. It wasn't surprising she'd shut her eyes to it so far, because of the pain it caused. Noel had met Nerida at Noel's Den. Noel's Den was the starting-point of the decay inherent in Noel's character. It was there that his pre-arranged plot with Don about the Peninsula trip had been sprung on Geraldine as a whim. It was there he'd nurtured a nasty dubious relationship with Dennis to the detriment of their own. Noel's Den was the cause of his continuing absence. It was where he'd given up respectability to run a dive with meals as cover for who knew what. Noel's Den was being enlarged and embellished. Noel all but lived at Noel's Den. Noel's Den was the scene of the real battle.

Noel had put Nerida in Geraldine's place already and wanted it literally true.

Noel's share in Noel's Den was more properly Geraldine's, because it was the cushion of her money behind him that gave him the courage to take the plunge at all. Why not dress up, Mrs McIntyre said. The pool reflected Mrs Mac's wisdom. Mrs Mac wasn't blind; she knew what was going on. She was worried today because, being her hair day, she must leave soon after lunch to keep her appointment. Plainly her worry was growing at Geraldine's increasing absorption and, being the sort of woman she was her thoughts would leap to suicide. Dear Mrs Mac – it was the last thing in Geraldine's mind. Geraldine would get the woman something nice to show how much she cared while on her way to giving Noel a nice surprise.

Win out at Noel's Den and the reasoning talk would follow and all else would fall into place. The thought was clear as the water below: take the offensive, win the battle on Noel's own ground.

Excited at the simplicity of it, Geraldine went inside. She poked her head in the kitchen. 'You're absolutely right, Mrs Mac, I'll do exactly that.'

Mrs McIntyre beamed round from the salad ingredients. 'You won't be here for your lunch then, dear.'

'No. Shove it in the fridge if there's too much. It'll keep till later.'

'Have a nice time.'

Geraldine ran upstairs. Poor old Noel panted up sometimes like an old bull walrus. Under the shower she had a funny dual sort of feeling – both fear and confidence. She was superior to the monotonous girls of today; youth wasn't everything. They, too, would grow old. She knew she meant only Nerida. There was certainly no challenge to her in Nerida's intellect.

Dress up, Mrs Mac said. Geraldine put on a longish dark brown silk thing, quite plain, beautifully cut, terribly expensive, stunning with her tawny hair and deep suntan. Bright pink lipstick, even her eyes touched up. Bag and shoes in a kind of mustardy yellow. The girl smiling back from the glass looked extraordinarily lovely, no more than a girl, no panic showing.

She went downstairs slowly. Mrs McIntyre would peer at her from the glassed patio. She got in the car she so rarely used and went out the front way. She needed no excuse to pop in at the Den, but had one in the extension.

On the way she stopped at a little shop she liked and got Mrs McIntyre a beautiful bowl from Sweden in thick clouded glass. Mrs McIntyre looked at beautiful bowls and sometimes indulged in plastic or cut-glass from chain stores.

More old houses had been done up. It all looked somehow shabbier. Noel's Den on its strategic corner looked to her the shabbiest of all, with Dennis's shrubs grown big enough to collect the passing dust. There were some parked cars. It was just after twelve-thirty. A blast of amplified music made Geraldine recoil. It all looked exactly the same, but when she got inside it was bigger. A wall had been knocked down to double the size, the whole area unified by a poisonous decor of geometric shapes in primary colours. That would be Dennis's designing genius. Hardly a place for restful eating, but the last thing these shouting people wanted was rest. A new bar ran the length of one wall.

There was one vacant chair at a table with two girls. The menu said spaghetti bolognese and veal cutlets. Geraldine wasn't hungry, just desperate. A waitress, another innovation, a pretty, slummocky girl about seventeen, took her order of a roll and coffee. Then Nick the waiter swung through from the kitchen with a high-held tray, and his trained gimlet eyes saw Geraldine. They opened wide, then the smile came. Soon after, Noel's head came round the swing door. He grinned and waved and made urgent signs.

Had she hoped to see Nerida?

Noel arrived just after the roll and coffee. 'Lovely surprise, goddess.' Just as Mrs McIntyre predicted. 'Don't you look ravishing. Like the new look?'

'It's lovely, darling.'

'Must get back. That all you're having? Don't run off, come back and see the kitchen, whole lot of improvements there too.'

'I'd love to.'

The coffee was good. Geraldine had a second cup. Perhaps the food was good. A bunch of people waited at the door for tables.

Now for the first time she saw men's and women's rooms in the far wall of the added room. Their doors were discreetly part of the geometric dazzle, just a medium M and W dead centre. Geraldine sat on until nearly two o'clock when the eaters were thinning out. Then she moved.

She heard Dennis's voice as she went through the swing door. 'I didn't know those people with the avocado tree's uncle was a supplier of ours.'

'Told you a thousand times,' Noel said.

'Geraldine!' Dennis slid off the bench where he'd been sitting and flung his arms round her in a nice imitation of welcome. Geraldine went stiff but kept her smile, and Dennis's hug turned flabby and died away.

Noel launched into what they'd done but Geraldine scarcely listened. She could see that here was the largest extension, a long kitchen about three times its former size and organised to cater for an increased clientele. And a chef with Noel's Den on his tall hat and a chef's assistant, Italian or Greek, and both grinning with pleasure.

'My wife,' Noel said with pride.

And two girls decoratively draped, one of them Nerida.

'Hi, Mrs Blaine,' Nerida said, 'don't often see you round here.'

Geraldine went on smiling, went on with admiring noises. No, Nerida was no challenge intellectually. The other girl was Gracie Something, dark curly hair, tinkling clothes, bare feet, merry dark eyes in a very small face. Faces getting smaller. At the other end the door opened on to the yard. Air-conditioning was here as in the restaurant.

'It's splendid, darling,' Geraldine's face ached with the smile. 'How long's it been finished?'

'Still needs a few touches,' Noel said, 'but been in operation about a fortnight.'

'Nice to have your approval,' Dennis said in his sardonic tone of ambivalence. 'What I mean is – we've watched it inch by inch but you get the total picture in one go.'

'Yes, I do.' I get the total picture. 'What about publicity?' she asked, 'with all your connections you could get a plug on television, couldn't you?'

'No need, angel,' Noel said. 'Word of mouth's best, and there's almost too much of that – and we had the wine campaign, remember.'

Nick and the two waitresses were going in and out. Nick seemed to handle the money too. Another male person came in from the back yard, an old man, and started rinsing and stacking dishes for the dishwasher. Quite a staff. Noel seemed superfluous. There was someone for everything. Dennis for management. What lie would Noel produce if she taxed him on the question?

Geraldine sat on a stool. They saw she was going to stick around. Nerida and Gracie said they must be off. It was after two-thirty.

'You must have an indulgent employer?' Geraldine smiled at Nerida.

Nerida shrugged. 'Gave it away after Chrissie,' she said casually.

Ah! And Noel keeps you?

Nick pushed the door. 'Fellow out there from Champion's, Mr Blaine, wants to see you.'

'Damn,' Noel said, moving towards Nick. Then he turned to Dennis. 'You know more than I do about his muck-up, Den. How about some moral support?'

They followed Nick from the kitchen.

'Coming, Gracie?' Nerida said. 'See you,' she tossed at Geraldine.

'When?' Geraldine put on her big warm smile. 'Let's fix a time, dinner one night, or what about Sunday, lunch and a swim? Are you doing anything Sunday?'

Nerida shrugged. 'Not specially. Sunday's okay.'

'Eleven, say?' Is eleven all right?'

'Okay.'

The girls went through the swing door as Dennis came back. Geraldine shut her eyes. She could feel Dennis's. The bustle and clatter all around her seemed to come from a great distance. She knew when the swing door was Noel and smiled at him. He looked at her, then at Dennis, then back at Geraldine.

'Should've had the spaghetti, goddess. They say it's the best ever, Italian to the core.'

'Next time, darling, I promise.'

'You shoving off now?'

'I thought I'd wait for you.'

'Well, there's tonight yet, dinner's wackier than lunch.'

Geraldine looked about pointedly, including Dennis in the summation. 'But everything's so organised. Surely one less body cluttering the kitchen would make for a smoother operation.'

'Well – ' Noel stopped. He looked at Dennis. Couldn't he make a decision without Dennis's approval?

'Push off, old chap,' Dennis said in a low voice, and there seemed to Geraldine in tone and words a secret understanding between them; a private reassurance from Dennis to deal with any commitments Noel might have later. Such as Nerida.

'Right, then,' Noel said, not hiding his reluctance.

All the same it wasn't till about four o'clock that he found he could get away. Geraldine waited and waited. She knew that ploy of his and knew she could outsit, outwait, outlast anything.

On the way Noel said, 'Slow down, angel, for God's sake.'

'You're joking.'

'You're whizzing too fast in all this traffic.'

Geraldine laughed and honked at the car in front. 'You, of all people!'

'That was the bad old days; not any more. Danger to life and limb. As a matter of fact I'd like to pack in cars altogether.'

'Have I got the wrong man in my car?' Geraldine was so suddenly happy she could burst.

'Jesus, goddess, the pollution. Kills off trees and birds – and us, to boot.'

Geraldine laughed again. 'You're a great little do-gooder all of a sudden.'

'Not sudden.'

'Really?'

After a pause Noel said, 'How about you, why don't you take an interest, angel? It's easy to get – well – sort of shut off from things.'

'What things?'

'Well, everything – the world.'

'You mean I'm shut off?'

Noel said, 'Shut in, perhaps.'

'Well, darling, who's to blame for that?' She waited for him to say the she herself was but Noel said nothing.

At home Geraldine put Mrs Mac's gift on the hall table. She wanted the talk to continue. 'Drink, darling?' she said.

'Love one.'

When they were out by the pool with their drinks Geraldine said, 'I think the Den looks marvellous, I really do.'

'Pretty good, isn't it?'

'They look a good staff.'

'Bang on.'

'Then surely you don't have to spend so much time there, darling?'

'Well, there's a helluva lot to do – it's hard to explain – things just go on cropping up like this business today with Champion's, an order they claim was delivered we never got. Believe me, angel, I'm not fooling.'

'And I'm not a child. It could run like clockwork without you most of the time.'

Noel gloomed at his drink, swishing the ice about. The sky was a bluey-gold.

Geraldine shivered. 'I'd like you with me more,' she said in a soft voice. Her hands itched to smooth his hair.

Noel drained his glass and stared at the pool.

'She's coming to lunch Sunday and a swim,' Geraldine said.

'Mm?' he looked at her. 'Who?'

'She's a pretty girl,' Geraldine said. 'About eleven.' She got up and took his glass.

'Eleven what?'

'She's coming, silly. Another?' She turned away from the look in his eyes which doubtless he thought unfathomable.

His voice followed her. 'No, thanks.'

'I'll see what Mrs Mac can rustle up for dinner,' Geraldine called over her shoulder.

Mrs Mac was reading the paper in her glasses with her hairdo. She saw at once from Geraldine's face that her strategy had worked.

'Hair looks nice,' Geraldine said.

'Sometimes I ask myself is it worth it.'

'Well, it is,' Geraldine said severely with her smile. 'We're both here to dinner, can you fix something? Any old thing, I'd like to be waited on tonight.'

'Of course, dear. I'm pleased as punch *any time*.' Mrs Mac took her glasses off.

'Any old thing,' Geraldine repeated shyly from the door.

'Seven-thirty?'

'Right you are.'

Geraldine got refills and went outside again. Noel wasn't there. Perhaps he'd gone up for a shower. She put the drinks by the pool and ran upstairs. Noel wasn't anywhere. There was no point in hunting around downstairs because she could feel he was gone. Geraldine locked herself in the bedroom.

When Mrs McIntyre kept on knocking Geraldine cried out, 'Leave me alone.' At last the woman's entreaties stopped.

The gift in its purple paper stayed on the hall table. The drinks remained by the pool, warm, the ice long melted.

———

CHAPTER 13

Geraldine kept silent about Noel's trickery. On Friday morning she saw he'd had breakfast, and there were signs he'd bunked down on a settee. No sound had disturbed her sleep. Explanation or apology should come from him. When neither did she behaved as though nothing extraordinary had happened. So did Noel.

And so did Mrs McIntyre after the first sharp look at Geraldine's face. Geraldine gave her the purple gift but didn't stay for the gasps of delight. Since then everything had been as usual, with Noel out most of Friday and Saturday. As usual.

But he remembered about Sunday. Perhaps had laughed about it with the guest. Remembered the hour of arrival, hanging around outside looking spruce and host like. Geraldine had planned nice things to eat and she went out to Noel to talk about drinks.

'You know what Nerida likes, darling.'

'Anything that's going.'

Nerida was half an hour late in a taxi. She had on a cotton caftan in tawny browns with bare feet and a red towel. 'Hi,' she said.

Geraldine's calm was a mite blurred but she hung on to it. It was important that Noel make the comparison. They had a swim, then sat around with drinks before lunch. Couldn't Noel see the difference between Geraldine's olive green one-piece elegance and Nerida's scanty pink bikini vulgarity?

'All right if I call you Gerry?' Nerida asked in a shy voice.

'My name is Geraldine.'

Noel laughed and Nerida said, 'Some people call me Nerry.' Then to fill in Geraldine's silence she went on, 'They've done a fab job on the Den, haven't they?'

'Excellent.'

'See that old washer-upper? – he's got a new lease of life with that job of his.'

Noel said, 'Nerida found him, an old-age pensioner, one of her good works.'

'Makes me seethe,' Nerida said, 'people shoved off into limbo, but it's part of the whole lousy mess all over the world.'

Geraldine smiled. 'You're young to be so concerned.'

'Well, it's up to us kids, isn't it? What have the oldies done? Take analgesics.'

Geraldine hid her boredom and resentment behind the wide smile. 'Only rarely,' she said.

'No, I mean the way they're promoted and sold and doctors wagging their hypocritical heads over ruined kidneys.'

'Nerida's right,' Noel said in a solemn voice.

The new reforming zeal: Noel's about-face on cars: a social conscience picked up from Nerida who'd arrived in a polluting taxi. Geraldine wanted to laugh. Noel the liberal. Three cheers. And the same for Nerida. Parrot-crying new themes daily on our sick society. It was so thin and silly, yet Noel was enraptured, and it was this that Geraldine couldn't bear. The pleased proud look he had for Nerida.

Abruptly she stood up. 'Another swim, or lunch?'

'Lunch, I think, goddess. Want a hand?'

'No, thanks.' She wanted to run but kept her walk casual. In her head she heard Nerida's silly childish voice babbling on about Arabs and analgesics and Aborigines and atomic waste. Stupid lost causes, and cynical Noel pretending commitment just to satisfy his lust. What had Geraldine done to deserve this? Why must he wound her with Nerida? He bore an undying grudge for the vasectomy she'd urged for the world's good, yet applauded Nerida's ignorant ideals which undoubtedly would include zero population growth. The meaningless chatter filled the kitchen, shrill and distracting over the trays she arranged.

She took a deep steadying breath, then picked up the antipasto tray. A garden picnic, how nice, how glum. No voices, no talk. And then she saw them. Supine. Their two bodies side by side face down beside the pool, touching, far far too close, overlapping. The long and the short of it, a juxtaposition so right. So right together, can't imagine them apart. The lovebirds.

The golden day the grey of her darkest dreams.

I can see it's over.

Geraldine saw it was ended, this year was the death of her love. Nerida's year. Slippery Noel had dodged away at a place beginning with B. A pre-planned spot on the map.

'Darling, wine?' Her bright, friendly voice.

Noel started up. 'Sorry, angel, nearly dropped off, it's the sun.'

It would look a pleasant lunch party from a helicopter, or on film. Talk and laughter, good food and wine. And after that three supine bodies, Geraldine's separating Noel from Nerida. Then a lazy dip. And at long last Nerida saying she must be going, but making no move.

Someone else turned up later. It was around five. A tall fair man who was vaguely familiar. Geraldine gave him a warm smile.

When at last they were alone Noel said it had been a lovely day. Nerida thought so too, he said. 'You enjoy it, angel?'

'Lovely, darling.'

'Damn good grub you put on.'

They didn't want much dinner. Odds and ends on a tray, picking with their fingers, intimate and cosy, with the news on television. Geraldine wondered at her forbearance; a scream would be more appropriate.

Afterwards, cosily, they watched a movie. Noel gave her a comradely goodnight kiss.

CHAPTER 14

A loose tile in the patio floor. A window sticking in the spare bedroom. Scuff marks on some of the walls. A hinge off a kitchen cupboard. A depletion in glass and china. The garden raggedy. Upstairs an erratic cistern. And the dishwasher going funny sometimes, Mrs Mac said. Things Geraldine ordinarily couldn't wait to have remedied. The house was going to pot. Let it.

Mrs Mac could do nothing and gave up trying. Geraldine shut her ears to the woman's worries. The desperate year was going, the house could go with it.

One day Noel got home early, about ten, and was fairly kind with a hug and the remark that it was nice to be home.

Then he said, 'Angel, Mrs Mac says she's worried about a few things cracking up.'

'Does she?'

'Well, angel, don't you think we ought to get the dishwasher man? Then the cistern upstairs, she says.'

'It doesn't matter.'

'Of course it matters, I'll have a go at the cistern, have a look at it anyway.'

A stirring of anger. 'What a little fixer, when will you find the time?'

Noel dropped into an arm-chair. 'Anything wrong with now?'

Geraldine snapped, 'Leave it, just leave it alone.'

'Why, angel?' He leaned forward quickly and grabbed her left hand. 'What's the matter? The house, why, you've kept it like a bloody palace. What's come over you?'

'I don't care about the house,' Geraldine grated. Then with a swift movement she was on her knees beside him, clutching in a fierce embrace. '*Darling*, let's just be *happy* – just *happy!*'

Noel stroked her hair. A caress for a fractious dog. Geraldine tightened her grip. Sobs were a lump in her throat.

Noel said, 'I thought we *were* happy, pretty well. I thought we'd managed fairly well these months, since you came back. I'd an idea you'd done some thinking up there.'

The sheer gall of it swept grief back to anger. She let go and sat back on her heels. It was really too funny. If laughter weren't dead, she'd laugh at the polished boards under Noel's feet. Laugh at the Persian rug just beyond. I'd an idea you'd done some thinking. Oh, yes, she remembered very clearly all the thinking she'd done in the stuffy orange tent and stuck beside Don in the Land-Rover. It was Noel gone to seed, not her house. A house could be fixed up, and if other things were more pressing now a house could be done later. Nerida was pressing; Nerida with Noel. That was pressing.

About a week later, on a weekday, Noel arrived home at lunch-time with a few people. No warning. It was mid March. A tall fair man – Jim, she remembered. Clyde. Claire Sayers (Dennis's supposed fianceé). And Nerida. Nerida and Noel in the lead. Geraldine on her tummy beside the pool, head on arms, watching out of the tops of her eyes, thinking, Here come the lovebirds, so right together. A pretty, silly face like thousands of others.

'Hi, angel, don't mind, do you? Felt like a dip so we all came on from the Den.'

Clyde unsteady. Drinks all round. No, not the fair man. He didn't. Invading Geraldine's privacy, invading *her* place, taking her pool over. She sat with knees to chin and her arms round her legs. On sufferance in her own house, at her own pool.

Claire, Jim and Nerida in her pool. Clyde's loud drunken voice going on and on, earbashing Noel. Clyde wasn't a water baby. A whisky baby come for more. On and on.

' – can't go wrong in a protean market, the vertical corporation, but you know all that, and the pattern of development and I include increased consumers with the immigration policy so long as they don't bugger it, I don't see it's a painful decision with the upswing of greater investments and property assets and debentures on the up and up; it's a major contribution on industry's part to the well-being of the nation *per se*.' Or something like that, because Geraldine's concentration was on Nerida's pretty body climbing out. The others were at the other end.

Then it happened. Clumsy, drunken, purple-faced Clyde got up to illustrate a point or maybe go to the loo to release some overflow, and his elbow swinging caught Nerida's pretty face and in she toppled, backwards.

Geraldine was up in a flash and swift and straight she dived in. Nerida was under. Geraldine brought her up. The girl struggled and spluttered, dazed with the blow. Alone, she might have drowned. A paddler, not a swimmer. Geraldine's instant reflexes saved her life. Geraldine's strength lifted Nerida to Noel's and Jim's hands. The Geraldine levered herself out. Nerida was brushing the sympathisers off, holding her face and head.

'I'm all right,' she said in a small voice.

'You're bloody marvellous, goddess,' Noel said. His face was white and looked old.

They all congratulated Geraldine. Claire was tiresome with sighs of relief. Clyde had flopped on the seat again. He was shaken and sick-looking; he seemed to be facing the emptiness of his life. His marriage over long ago, mad for Geraldine, drowning anguish in drink and economic conundrums.

Nerida caught at Geraldine's hand. She was crying. 'Thank you, I don't know what – ' She couldn't go on.

Geraldine swung to the pool and dived in. She gave a display of diving and swimming, showed off all her tricks, concentrating on perfection, feeling her face set in a mask even while she breathed in and expended air. Unseeing, she saw their admiration. Her mind was intent on something else: anger. At last she swam lazily to one side of the pool and got out. The fair man was there; he'd been the keenest observer. He seemed nice. Sober, quiet. She wondered where Noel met him.

'Magnificent,' he said with a shy smile.

Geraldine shrugged, then wished she hadn't. Nerida was the shrugger. 'You don't seem to fit with the others. What do you do?'

'I'm with a firm of accountants.'

Ah, through Clyde.

'I hope you'll change you mind about Cape York,' he said.

Geraldine gave him a nice smile. 'Thanks, but no,' she said. They were all on sufferance, this man too. But especially Noel.

They hung around a bit longer, going over and over Nerida's shave that might have been so close, perhaps too close, without Geraldine's swift action. Repetitive talk, shouting each other down. Everyone a false face, herself too. If I had friends, Geraldine thought, they'd be nice big silent animals like hippopotamuses that go silently about their business and never let me down.

They hung around till nearly four.

Geraldine was still by the pool when Noel got home just before midnight. It had been a hot still night, close and muggy. Mrs McIntyre had gone home shaking her stiff-haired head.

Geraldine had everything sorted out in her mind: what she'd say, what he'd say. It didn't go at all like that. No love, no gentleness, no give and take.

'Noel.'

Noel came from the carport. 'Jesus, goddess, you know the time?'

'Tell me the truth about Nerida.'

Noel stood stock still looking down at Geraldine where she sat on the poolside hugging her knees. She couldn't see the shiftiness in his eyes but she knew it was there.

Noel said slowly, 'If I told you the truth you'd – ' and stopped.

'I'm listening.'

'You just don't get it, do you, what you – the way you make people uncomfortable. Up the coast, Julie – '

'Julie!'

'Your crazy jealousy buggers everything, everyone sees, they know that smile's not real – '

'People are fools.'

'People's all there is.'

'*People*, who cares? It's *us* I'm talking about.'

Noel moved, shifting his lies about, picking them over as he paced away and then returned. 'There isn't any us. It's been over for years, and you know it.'

'Never before like Nerida.'

'You say that every time. It's been Dennis, Claire, Gail, Jill Munro, even Elaine, and all the others before the Den. Now it's Nerida.'

Geraldine said in a bleak voice, 'I know.'

'*In your mind.*'

'From when you met her, long before the trip.'

Noel shrugged, just as Nerida shrugged. 'I suppose I'm glad you've brought it up, I've been wanting a talk a long time.'

That was funny; it was a scream, after the accounting she'd sought with him so long ago. Geraldine raked the detritus over in her mind.

'Well, I'm off to bed,' Noel said, 'I'm just about buggered.'

But Geraldine moved swiftly and stood in his way. 'Try honesty. Tell me you want that run-of-the-mill tramp. Tell me you've been trying to break my spirit so I'd give in.'

'Jesus, angel, don't have a fit at this hour.' Roughly he pushed past her and went into the house, leaving Geraldine to extrapolate the truth she knew: Nerida was it for keeps.

She stared into the pool, wishing its bright turquoise dark and murky. She knew this downwards sensation. It was sinking into deep dark water and not being able to swim, even to struggle. It cut her off from life.

It was a long time before Geraldine went inside, but in the morning her mind was a blank, all of yesterday a blur that meant nothing.

The blurriness remained, a world where hurt couldn't reach. Geraldine put the repairs and replacements in hand and Mrs McIntyre made daily sounds of approval. Noel came home at night and slept in her bedroom in his bed and left again in the mornings. He spoke sometimes in a neutral voice about clean socks and had she seen his keys and sometimes the weather.

After a boisterous wet April, May came in warm and muggy. It meant the pool again, the pool that was all her refuge. Nerida liked the pool too and was serious about want-ing to learn to swim, above all to feel confident in the water. She'd come a few times during April but mostly they had to stay inside, although Nerida loved the house and never tired of admiring Geraldine's things. Nerida was a nice girl, of course young and silly, no depth, but generous and warm-hearted, with a praiseworthy concern for the world's evils. Nerida said they could all be put right, that all it needed was everyone getting behind them. Geraldine loved Nerida's enthusiasm. Nerida's over-riding preoccupation was gratitude and that was her biggest enthusiasm. So grateful to Geraldine for her life. During May Nerida came more often. It was so lovely by the pool, just the two of them, sheltered from the winds and people. Noel smiled a lot, although sometimes he looked worried, almost scared.

Jim came one day out of the blue. His second name was Oates. The three of them had fun in the pool and Jim thought

Nerida's swimming was coming along fine. He said his Cape York trip was organised to set off earlyish in July.

The weather in May was best of the year, clear and sunny but not too hot. Nerida never came without being invited by Geraldine. The first time had resulted from her telephone call to Geraldine to say she'd never forget how wonderful Geraldine had been in the pool that day. 'Everything went a black fuzz,' she said. 'Maybe one of the others would have fished me out, but I'm glad I didn't have to rely on it.' Geraldine said nonsense and invited her over, and then went on inviting the poor rudderless thing.

———

CHAPTER 15

Until one lovely June morning Nerida came uninvited. In bare feet, by taxi.

Geraldine hadn't planned a day alone, nothing so definite, yet felt in a vague way that this had been her intention. Sunning on the edge, delicious after the day's cold start, and plunging in when she felt like it.

'Okay with you?' Nerida asked casually. A formality, not a question. 'Noel invited me.'

'Oh.' Geraldine smiled by stretching her lips. 'He's not here, I'm afraid.' Then the lie, 'He phoned, something urgent cropped up, something Dennis couldn't handle.' There was always something urgent at Noel's Den.

'Too bad,' Nerida said. 'What a fabulous day.'

'He should have let you know,' Geraldine said. She stared at Nerida's bare feet and felt a tiny explosion of anger. 'Let's have a swim anyway. It's lovely in, coldish but I like that. D'you want to ring Noel first?'

Nerida laughed her careless laugh. 'Mustn't interrupt affairs of state.'

Just my marriage, my life.

Geraldine's swimsuit, a black one, was still damp. She stood up as Nerida dropped her caftan thing – always the same one, a bit grubby – and then dived beautifully. She rose slowly, rolled over and looked back. And there was Nerida, topless, just a bikini brief, a mere thread of pink, that lovely body, neat and small, brown all over, skin with a sheen, the small exciting breasts that roused Geraldine in a way the wouldn't be Noel's way. All in one paralysing moment.

Geraldine swam back with lazy strokes. Nerida was pretending to limber up. Showing off her young, compact body, preening her triumph over an old, spent, used-up woman. Thirty-one wasn't old. Geraldine was out of the pool in one lithe movement of shining wet limbs and sparkling drops.

'Ready?' she asked, smiling.

Together they dived in, Geraldine automatically shortening her reach as she had during Nerida's lessons. They were level under water. And then it was happening so naturally, effortlessly, it was so right, so inevitable. Geraldine was deeper, she was so much stronger, she would see, plan, manipulate, she was in control. Catching hold of Nerida's wisp of bikini, pulling her down, holding her closer, strong hand cruelly gripped between Nerida's legs at that hated junction. With a deep satisfaction, a spreading peace. Nerida struggled for breath, she had none, unprepared, her mouth open, the first wild panic weakening. Geraldine surfaced, still holding Nerida's bikini, putting all her strength into her rigid arm, taking air she scarcely needed. A look at the silent loneliness. No Noel, Mrs McIntyre upstairs intent with the vacuum cleaner. Geraldine lunged below again. It was something that had to be done, a riddance. She felt no malice now, felt nothing at all, only release. It was as if she applauded in silence while somebody else performed this necessary act. Strange to feel so remote and yet be so practical. Dear little dead face, like the flying fox shot by Don.

When Geraldine came back up she was alone. She got out slowly, feeling dreamy. Without hurry she picked up her towel and went into the patio. Her sandals were there. She looked back. Only Nerida's caftan, a limp heap of tawny browns, and her scarlet towel.

Geraldine went upstairs. The vacuum cleaner's whirr was soothing. After locking the bedroom door she hung her swimsuit and towel to dry in the bathroom. Then she dressed in woolknit pants and a cashmere sweater. She'd wanted to break it up between them, but death hadn't entered her head. How simple it was. There'd be no marks; it had been accomplished via the bikini and Nerida's panic.

She pulled the curtains to darken the room and placed aspirin and water on the bedside table. Then she lay down with a damp cloth over her eyes. Months of tension had given her headaches, and black smudges under her eyes bore witness to a headache that was now wonderfully vanished. She lay without moving but not relaxed because inside elation bubbled. Lying down on the brink of a high was a new experience she liked. Everything was such fun: the telephone when it rang three times and stopped, then Mrs Mac's gentle single knock on her door; the remote swooping whine of a jet, excitement up in her throat; then again later the telephone. But Mrs Mac didn't knock again because she knew about Geraldine's headaches. The vacuum cleaner had stopped long ago.

Then at last Noel came. A more peremptory knock, lacking the woman's compassion, *en grand seigneur*. Geraldine called a weak reply, got up pressing the towel to her head and opened the door to him. Even as he spoke she tottered back to the end and lay down again.

'Head's bad, is it? Mrs Mac said on the phone it was.'

'Don't shout, darling.'

'You hear the phone? I rang twice.'

Geraldine moved her head a fraction in the negative.

'Nerida come?'

Another tiny negative, then in a low voice she said, 'I don't know, I heard nothing, no bells.'

Noel sat on the side of her bed and Geraldine winced at the movement. Noel got up again.

'Sorry,' he said. 'Thing is, I asked Nerida for a swim today and forgot about telling you.'

Geraldine sighed, her eyes shut.

'Then this stupid business cropped up.'

Geraldine smiled faintly. 'Doesn't it always?'

'Point is I forgot to ring her and put it off.'

'You *are* forgetful, darling.'

Noel paced about and then came back. 'I tried to ring Nerida at her place, but she was out, so I guessed she'd be here.'

Geraldine sighed. 'Have you looked?'

'Well, she can't be, I'd have seen her.'

Geraldine turned her head tiredly away from him, indicated that was that.

'You had a swim today?' Noel said.

Geraldine sighed again and said with an effort, 'An early one, I thought it might fix my head, but it was too bad already and then the sun.' Her head slumped sideways again then, as though so many words had used up her strength.

'Poor old thing, no better?' Noel put his hot hand on her forehead and Geraldine flinched from it.

'It'll go in time, with quiet.'

'I'll stick around downstairs, goddess. No point in going back now; it's okay with Dennis. Maybe she'll turn up, I'll try ringing again.'

None of this interested Geraldine and she made no reaction.

'Think you could cope with a spot of lunch by the pool? I'll root around with Mrs Mac and fix up the big umbrella.'

'All right, darling. You just fix it all and let me know.'

The fool patted her hair and tiptoed to the door. He went out and shut it gently behind him.

Geraldine was still on the bed when Noel came back some time later. He knocked and came in on tiptoe. Geraldine opened her eyes and removed the towel. Noel came over and looked down at her.

'Thought you might have dropped off. Any better?'

'A teeny bit, so long as all stays quiet.' She sat up holding her head, then got up. 'Shan't be a sec, darling.'

She started for the bathroom as Noel said, 'I can't make it out.'

Geraldine went into the bathroom and when she came out ten minutes later Noel was still there, slumped on the side of her bed. He looked up at her.

'She's still not there. I don't get it. She'd have let me know.'

'It's nothing to do with me, darling.' Geraldine brushed her hair. 'Why don't the two of you sort it out later? Lunch ready?'

'Sure.'

They went downstairs. Geraldine felt wonderfully calm. Noel said he'd bring lunch out, no need to trouble Mrs Mac.

Geraldine went out to the pool. She could see it, down the other end. She put on hr dark glasses and sat languidly on the swing-seat, waiting with closed eyes. She heard him coming.

'Here we are, goddess.' Steaming bowls of soup, crackers, cheeses, hearts of celery. 'Enough for you?'

'Heavens yes, darling, lovely. Out of a can?'

'The basis. Enriched with sour cream, chives and things.'

'You *are* clever.'

Noel had claret, a whole bottle he'd opened. Behind his pleasantness Geraldine could see his worry. How strange that he'd sit here getting stinking while the cause bumped gently against the other end of the pool. It looked so small.

It wasn't till they'd finished eating and Noel on his third glass of claret was thinking of getting the coffee that he saw it.

'What's that?'

'What, darling?'

Noel stood up. 'I thought – Jesus!' he crashed the glass down and raced along the side of the pool.

Geraldine stood up holding her head. 'What on earth – '

But Noel was hauling the body out. Geraldine walked along the side towards him. He was crying, trying at the same time to effect respiration. Hands all over Nerida's torso, on her naked breasts. Then he tried the kiss of life, only it wasn't, it was the demented kiss of passion. Geraldine stooped down and pulled at him gently.

'Darling, surely you can see it's too late.'

For a moment more he knelt over Nerida's body, his head bent down to her, his tears falling unchecked. Then he turned his head and looked at Geraldine with such an expression – so many things: hatred, doubt, accusation, distrust, anger, contempt. Geraldine stared back and knew in that instant it was Noel who ought to have died. Darling Noel.

'How absolutely dreadful,' Geraldine said.

Noel got up and ran inside. Noel the betrayer, far worse than silly Nerida, because Noel knew what he was doing to Geraldine. Geraldine stood up again and waited as if in prayer.

'The doctor's coming.'

Geraldine turned to him and removed her glasses. Her eyes held tears. 'Darling, come away, leave it to him.' His gaze was riveted on Nerida and it was an effort to make him move. Then just as they got to the swing-seat she clutched his arm. 'Look, darling, what's that? Isn't it Nerida's?'

Noel started towards the caftan and towel, but Geraldine's voice pulled him up short. 'I don't think we ought to touch anything.'

Noel came back, slumped down and poured some wine.

'Did you tell Mrs Mac?'

He shook his head. No. Then he said in a puzzled voice, 'Nerida was a good swimmer.'

'Not really, darling.'

'Not in your class, but adequate.'

But Geraldine knew that water to Nerida was a strange and frightening element. Not, as it was to Geraldine, familiar as air.

'Funny she should come and just use the pool,' Noel said.

'I thought you said you asked her.'

Noel was silent a moment. 'But when I wasn't here – didn't she come and hunt you out?'

'Darling, stop tormenting yourself – no, she didn't, no one's allowed that liberty except you. She might have seen Mrs Mac.'

'It's damned funny.'

'There's no point saying the same thing over and over.'

'No, I mean – it's not like you to flake out, just at the same time.'

'How would you know when I flake out? You're never here.'

Noel got up with his glass and went inside. A few minutes later he came back followed by Mrs McIntyre. Above her white face her hair was a shock, the same colour as Noel's claret. She took a quick look at the distant lifeless body then turned her back on it.

'Oh my goodness, to think of it and us both inside, dear.'

'Yes, it's horrible,' Geraldine said.

'I told Mr Blaine, I never knew nothing about her being here.'

'Of course not, I'm sure you didn't.'

The doctor came then. He looked at the rigid girl, asked the obvious questions and got the negative replies. He made a quick examination there and then and seemed more puzzled than anything. Geraldine, holding her head, insisted on staying, although Mrs Mac said she ought to go and lie down again, poor thing.

The doctor rang the police and came back outside. He said there were no apparent marks. Then he got their individual stories. Mrs McIntyre's was patently innocent. Geraldine's fell into the same category: an early plunge, and then lying down all morning with a bad head, knowing nothing of Noel's invitation to Nerida: a fact Noel had to confirm. After this it was Noel's story that sounded funny because the doctor gave him a shrewd and funny look.

They went over all of it again for the two policemen when they came. There was no one to back up Noel's story, but Mrs McIntyre did wonders for Geraldine.

'Well, see, Mrs Blaine gets these awful headaches, I see 'em; they've been bad in the last year. I know she came out here early, but she wasn't here when I happened to glance out, so she must've come in, that's for sure. Besides, when Mr Blaine rang twice the poor thing had her bedroom door locked.'

Nerida was taken away.

Just after four-thirty the phone rang. It was for Geraldine. It was Jim Oates, trying for the last time to get Geraldine to change her mind about joining his Cape York safari. 'I've got some nice kids coming,' he said, 'six of them. You and I would make eight in all.'

The man was a pest. 'I said no and meant it. I hope you have a nice time.'

She stared at the wall. The Peninsula. The point she thought she'd reached at last today. And then been faced with the real one. Her head was full of fur.

A full examination of the body established drowning as the cause of death. There was no injury, no mark or sign of a blow, no organic illness acute or chronic. The young lady wasn't pregnant, and in any case as a reason for suicide pregnancy was not what it used to be. The young lady must have panicked, there appeared no other reason for even a non-swimmer to drown in such an area of water. Two plain-clothes detectives arrived and went over everything again. They said it was unsatisfactory but not unprecedented. Death was a funny thing, they said. An unexplained death was always unsatisfactory. They said the girl's parents weren't vengeful, just sad; they'd known their daughter was good at heart and would very soon settle down. They concentrated more on Noel because of his dubious story, their grave faces implying that without Noel's streak of forgetfulness the girl might still be alive. Mostly they left Geraldine alone, because she too was a victim of Noel's forgetting. Geraldine didn't pay them much attention: look-alike dull kind men, dumb oxen.

Then they left too and everything was the same as it was before Nerida. Just herself and Noel, and Noel's Den.

Except it wasn't the same, was it? Both a year older. No parties. Nobody came. Above all, Noel stayed home a lot, often not even going to Noel's Den, watching Geraldine, his puzzlement turned to a silent and brooding accusation. Nerida was as alive as ever.

CHAPTER 16

Soon after that Noel ran off the road in his car, in the dark.
Poor Noel. A common accident, people did it a lot, mostly
young, late at night after drinking. Noel had been drinking, even though he was not as young as he'd like to be.
He'd been drinking a lot since Nerida. He couldn't snap
out of Nerida. He'd changed a lot, grown introspective, as
though there were something on his mind he couldn't
shake off. Noel, of all people. Noel, who said who cares? to
just about everything. So gloomy, never a pun, no careless
hugs or empty-headed laughter. He followed Geraldine
about as if seeking comfort in companionship, but
Geraldine knew it wasn't comfort he was after. He lay
awake for hours night after night; he even got some sleeping-pills from the doctor. Noel, of all people, who'd so
derided pill-takers.

Then suddenly he thought perhaps he'd take a trip somewhere, a complete change of scene. He asked Geraldine to go
with him; he said it would be good for both of them and dull
the tragedy. He said they really needed each other now.
They'd been drifting apart too long. This might be the
answer. Geraldine didn't even laugh. The Peninsula popped
into her head, but she didn't even laugh. Instead she put on a
grave face and said perhaps he was right. She'd think about it.

Then Noel came home one day and said he'd broached
the idea to Dennis, and Dennis was all for it. Dennis said fine,

go ahead, we'll manage. Noel urged Geraldine again. He couldn't bear to go alone, he said.

'Besides, it might give you a fresh outlook too, goddess, stop you brooding so much.'

Geraldine kept a straight face and agreed a change seemed a good idea. Idly she wondered whether Jim Something would like Noel along on his safari in her place; after all, it was Noel's tall tales that had got Jim going. The idea amused her but she said nothing.

'Yes, darling, of course,' she said.

So Noel hurled himself into organising. He planned an itinerary though Victoria and South Australia, made motel bookings, cancelled deliveries for six weeks, gave Mrs Mac the dates, got his car checked. Happy to be taking positive steps towards leaving behind the vacuum of Nerida.

Not a thought for the emptiness in Geraldine's life.

Of course, he consulted her about every detail, just as he had before plunging into Noel's Den. It was one of the things that made Noel so lovable, this pretence of joint decisions. But what did he have in mind? He was baffled by Nerida's death; he couldn't somehow picture what had happened. Did he hope to go over and over it in motel rooms until at last Geraldine remembered forgotten detail? Or did he plan direct action?

Geraldine felt strange during this period, neither up nor down; in a way suspended. On the surface she was able to fuss over Noel, enthuse about his tour plans and sort out what he'd need to take. The last day was a bustle for both of them. Mrs Mac prepared an enormous dinner because 'you can't drive on an empty stomach', and then went home. She'd be back in the morning to clear up.

Then right at the last minute, all ready to leave (Noel liked night driving), Geraldine thought a final drink would be nice. He'd just come swaying in from the carport, and Geraldine caught him and snuggled against him, face uplifted, arms tight round him.

'A toast to fair weather ahead, darling.' Noel had had quite a lot already, before dinner, during and since.

'Lovely thought, angel. Get them while I stow these?' He scooped up Geraldine's knee rug, grabbed her umbrella and make-up case and his own camera gear and binoculars, and loaded like a silly donkey staggered through the patio to the carport.

Geraldine got the drinks, a mild Scotch and water for herself, a big brandy for Noel.

When he came back, she saw that the misery had started up. Drink did it to him, showed him his stark loss. Geraldine gave him a lovely smile and handed him his glass. 'Clear skies, darling,' she said.

It was while they were drinking the toast, Noel white and tense on the settee with the heartbreak he didn't hide that Geraldine said softly she'd changed her mind.

Noel stared, looking silly.

'There's no point, darling. After all we can't leave ourselves behind, can we? We're stuck with us wherever we go.'

Noel got up in a rage. He glared at her and then at his glass, then drained it. 'Never bloody unwind, can you?' The glass broke when he hurled it across the room. He rushed out blindly through the patio.

Geraldine sat on quietly in her arm-chair, not finishing her own drink. She could hear thumps and smashes and slurred imprecations. Then soon the car starting up and going off in a maddened sort of way. After some minutes of total silence Geraldine went through to the carport and in two trips brought her things back inside. She'd known Noel would throw them all out anyhow in his violence. She knew Noel so well. She picked up the pieces of broken glass, wrapped them up in a sheet of the *Australian* and tucked them in the pedal bin in the kitchen. After unpacking and putting everything away she had a bath and went to bed.

But sleep wouldn't come, and a furriness in her head made reading impossible. Because Noel was doomed to crash. She took two of her sleeping-pills, the first she'd ever needed, and very soon was asleep. She didn't hear anything until the next day.

The police brought the news. Mrs Mac had the dish-washer going. Mrs Mac wasn't a bit surprised at Geraldine's change of mind about the car tour. 'On again, off again, dear, packing and unpacking. You had enough of that last year, you told me.'

The policeman was very gentle in the living-room. Death had been instantaneous. Her husband had had far too much to drink, well over the safety level, and further examination would be made to determine whether there'd been any con-tributing factor.

Geraldine wiped her eyes. 'Conscience, perhaps,' she said.

The policeman pricked up his ears.

'I just mean – well, he might have planned it.' She felt far away, watching somebody else sit through the policeman's stupidity. Her voice was low. 'He was very disturbed, in a way crazy with grief. A girl drowned here in the swimming-pool not long ago and my husband was very – ' she stopped a sob with her handkerchief. 'He was very fond of her,' she said in a rush.

'Well, we'll see,' the policeman said, in water deeper than he'd expected.

'He's been drinking a lot, taking sleeping-pills.'

'You'd better get some rest,' the policeman said in a kind voice. 'We'll see about the other later.'

He left with a lot to think about. Geraldine went weeping to the kitchen. Mrs Mac was beside herself when she heard the dreadful news. She said the most comforting thing she could think of.

'Thank God you changed your mind, dear.'

Geraldine went through the ells in the telephone book. Lemmon? Lemming? Then realised it was Noel's Den she wanted. She found it under Restaurants and told Dennis the sad news. Dennis was horrified but somehow not astonished.

'He's been terribly low. Ghastly for you, Gerry. You know, when something happens to happy people like Noel, they take it harder, I think. Anything I can do just let me know. Any time.'

'Thank you.'

'Don't worry about the Den.'

'Thank you.'

There was her share of the Den she had to be rid of. Dennis might like to buy it, Clyde could attend to that. How funny it was, poor darling Noel dead. Trusting her right to the end, right to his dying moment. As she'd trusted him while he sneaked back to Sydney and Nerida.

Three detectives came, quite a crowd. All big men with pale eyes. Saxon and Wells, and Thingummy in the kitchen with Mrs Mac. She told Saxon and Wells about the drinking and the sleeping-pills. They knew. She told them about the staying out till all hours. They hadn't known that.

'He was so upset at her death,' Geraldine said.

'That's the drowned girl, Nerida Jessop?'

'I don't think he was in love with her, or anything, it was just her youth and energy and – no inhibitions, that sort of thing.'

'He made double bookings at motels.'

'Well, poor darling, he hoped till the last minute I'd go, although all along I'd said I wouldn't. That sort of thing's so tiring.'

'He cancelled deliveries for six weeks.'

They'd been busy. Geraldine looked sadder. 'He was very impulsive.'

'His partner, Mr Lemmon, understood you were going.'

'The same thing.' Geraldine sighed. 'Noel hoped he could make it true.' How silly they were with their remote and meaningless questions.

They talked about the body. Geraldine declined to see it. It wouldn't be the living Noel, she said, the man she would always love. Mr Lemmon had identified it, and he'd love to do the funeral too; he was dying to help.

They said it was most unusual to take an overdose of sleeping-pills and then set off in a car. Geraldine said everything was unusual and brought them back to Nerida. Such idiots not to see the connection.

'It might have been conscience,' she mused. 'I've gone over and over it all and it seems to stand out. Conscience or fear.'

'Fear?' They pounced on that.

'I mean – not physical fear – it was just that Nerida was so clinging, I suppose you could say she *dogged* him, and although of course he'd be mistaken to think it he might have thought if he lost me he'd, well, lose out on quite a lot, so perhaps – ' she stopped.

'Go on, Mrs Blaine.'

'I don't know whether I can say it – perhaps it was the only way to prise Nerida loose.'

They gave her grave looks. Poor Mrs Mac with Thingummy, how she'd hate it. One of them said, 'Are you suggesting Mr Blaine drowned her?'

'Heavens, no. All I meant – she was becoming a nuisance.'

Everything went into a notebook. It was odd to feel so serene. The longer they stayed, the more at peace she felt, the more she felt a sense of religious fulfilment.

After they'd gone she had a late lunch in the kitchen with Mrs Mac. Mrs Mac had again been a brick.

'I told whatever-his-name-is that Mr Blaine had been pestering you about going away, dear, and you being so good-natured he thought he'd get his own way, as usual. I told him about the lovely dinner I got, and said I didn't reckon Mr Blaine would eat any of it, not with the drinking he'd been doing all day.'

Mrs McIntyre chattered on, concerned at Geraldine's sad face. Behind the face Geraldine was thinking things out in the detective's shoes. Wasn't it likely that Noel had drowned Nerida, then in remorse or fear taken his own life? He had a strong motive in Geraldine's money. Everyone likes the cushion of more, particularly wayward people like Noel. Nerida was a determined clinger, a man-eater, and Noel had feared that Geraldine's tolerance would snap. His one thought was Geraldine's money and the easy life he could have, for ever idle, free of worry, so if Nerida wouldn't go quietly he had to make sure she did, quietly dispatch her himself. It fitted. It was plain and simple, and the simplest solutions were usually right, weren't they?

Mrs McIntyre went to the funeral. Everyone understood, she said, why Geraldine couldn't bring herself to go, sick with grief as she was. The flowers were lovely, she said.

Faye Hudson was the only one of the former crowd to phone. She and Walter were terribly upset, and she wondered would Geraldine like a strong shoulder. Geraldine said how sweet, but no. But everyone sent poisonous black-bordered envelopes.

It was the start of July. Unusually cold with frosty mornings. Was it only a year ago, a bit less, when she'd been so happy that early morning before they set off in the afternoon for the Peninsula? The still cold was the same. The high hopes she'd had. Space to breathe in, time to talk. What a fool. Well, they were together now, Noel and Nerida, just as they'd planned.

The detective called Saxon came again, and then the one named Wells. Separately. They weren't trying to catch her out, no breath of suspicion had touched her. It was because they hated loose ends. Neither death could be neatly filed away. They wanted to explain the inexplicable.

It was tiresome. They depressed Geraldine. Although they were kind enough, their persistence was a nuisance. Mrs McIntyre said it was like their cheek.

But they could find no loophole. Geraldine went over it all in her mind and knew there were no tangibles. Facts would remain hidden because there was nothing to establish them. She'd been clever about his sleeping-pills, reminding Noel to pack them. He was in no condition to notice the contents, just chucked the plastic container in his toilet case. Noel overlooked details. Her own bottle contained twenty-three, two less than the original prescription: the two she'd taken the night he drove off to kill himself. They knew Noel had taken a lot of sleeping-pills; they just didn't know they'd been in that last big brandy; and even if they narrowed it down, they could only assume he'd put them there himself. And if they were going to find that out they'd have done so already at the time of the autopsy. All the drink he'd had would seem to them sufficient reason alone for the crash. Drinking and driving were inextricably linked in police minds. Geraldine only had sleeping-pills at all because Noel had, because after Nerida died and Noel got some, Geraldine said how can I sleep if you don't? In a burst of belated compassion, he suggested he sleep in another room but Geraldine wouldn't hear of it. She preferred to have all of him, she said, so must share with him his sleeplessness and whatever else was troubling him. It had been easy to pull the capsules open and empty the contents on paper, then to funnel the paper into a little plastic jar. He trusted her so, right up to the end, right up to drinking the brandy and smashing the glass. As she'd trusted him when he ditched her for Nerida at some place beginning with B. She knew it would all work out exactly the way it had. The empty capsules she took to Double Bay that last morning while Noel was out kissing the Den goodbye. She dropped them in a litter bin on a busy corner crunched in a sheet of newspaper.

So the serenity should have stayed. Instead she was suddenly low, empty, feeling no joy and no despair, out of touch. Something was missing. Noel, of course, but there was something more that eluded her. Following the satisfaction of exacting justice there should be a new impetus, an involvement not dependent upon Noel. She missed him terribly. His loss made a different emptiness from the emptiness of Noel alive and hurting her. Noel had called her obsessed. Was loving someone obsession? Flimsy Noel had never loved. Even his greed and his lust were flimsy. She'd always had an ideal of Noel, and this she would always love. But how barren it was, barren and empty, only this lifelessness the obsession.

'You've got to snap out of it, dear,' Mrs McIntyre said. 'A plush hotel somewhere, that's what you need, do you a world of good. New Zealand say, lots of nice new people.'

It was then that the craziest, most unlikely thing popped into Geraldine's head. It was the date reminded her on top of Mrs Mac: the tall fair man's Peninsula trip. Perhaps he'd gone already. When had he said? What was his name? Jim. The other name? She remembered thinking mnemonically. Alien corn. Of course: Oates. The images returned, the overlapping details of the first trip, the confusion. Heat and insects, pitching and striking camp, the quarrels, and sweats, the living earth, all the scarcities, the oddities met on the way, strange juxtapositions. Human shortcomings revealed as proximity and harsh conditions stripped the veneer. Impressions tumbling so fast that thinking must be compressed into a little tent. Suddenly it all seemed terribly right and desirable. She wanted to be there again. It would be an escape, but a search too. This time really see the point of it all. A rounding-off with illusions dead and buried. No more Noel-obsessed mistakes.

She went to the phone. It was almost eleven at night. She leafed through the book and found his number. The phone ringing made her jump. Impatient to talk to Jim, with the ridiculous notion that he might leave during this silly call, she snapped an answer.

It was Jim Oates.

'It's crazy,' Geraldine said happily, 'I was just about to ring you.'

'I'm hoping you've changed your mind, Mrs Blaine.' He sounded different but it would be the hour and the dark.

'Oh, marvellous, that's what I wanted. I was going to ask is there still room for me, I wondered – '

'Like to have you along, we leave on the twelfth, okay?'

'Yes, of course. I suppose you've heard about – '

'Yes, I know. You know what to bring. You'll be travelling in my vehicle. I'll phone you the day before, okay?'

'Yes, and do you – '

'Fine. Goodnight.'

Businesslike, to say the least. Geraldine had been going to ask whether he advice were needed, since this had been the thing he'd stressed in the first place. Men were all a bit weird; people in general.

Next morning, told the decision, Mrs McIntyre said comfortably, 'I know just what you mean, dear, you don't know which way to turn.'

Less than a week. The flurry of getting ready. Geraldine was more excited than if she'd been off to Europe or somewhere with Noel.

Mrs Mac said, 'Now don't you worry about a thing, dear, everything's safe with me.' Mrs Mac was going to live in.

Jim rang as he'd promised. 'I'll pick you up at five sharp. We'll meet up with others and get going. All right?'

'I'll be ready.'

'I suppose you've got permission.'

'Permission?'

'Officially – weren't there enquiries?'

Geraldine took a big breath. 'Not enquiries, just establishing the few known facts.' Her voice was icy.

'Fine,' Jim said. 'See you in the morning.'

It was absurd. Geraldine knew how absurd it was yet still it threw that last day out of kilter. It meant there'd been malicious talk.

And going to bed she saw the new moon through glass. That was absurd, too.

Part three

Geraldine sat on a groundsheet under a leafy tree with big red flowers. Away from the tents but having them in sight. The others thought her an old square. Thirty-one wasn't old. Not when one had what she had. At her age what would they have? Nothing. They had nothing now, only youth they squandered. Where on earth had Jim dredged them up? Young people were – but the thought drifted off and away. Later she'd do her nails. When it got a bit cooler, around sunset. Jim was different, but he was older, a year younger then Geraldine. He'd changed a bit on the way up. He'd been nice enough at first, quietly comprehending her loss. Did everyone change on the way up to Cape York Peninsula? Look at Noel. Only Geraldine remained steadfast and sane.

They'd joined the coast at Townsville. They came up inland for some reason of Jim's. It didn't matter to Geraldine because getting away was all, sanctuary. Was it something to do with a Land-Rover? She'd had an impression of three to start with, and now there were four. Old ones; all tried and true, Jim said.

And now they were stuck in Cairns on the far north coast of Queensland. The delay irritated Geraldine; she wanted to keep moving. Idleness and humidity strangled mind and body: thought crept like a slug, limbs gave in to torpor. She wanted no more stalemates. Just to reach the end: attainment and perhaps some kind of atonement. But Jim was buying essentials like chains and a long jack, and at this late hour getting route details. All things she could have told him.

There were ways she might fill up time: swims in the turquoise sea, walks, tours. She could have gone with the others yesterday to some commercial fauna reserve: crocodiles, brolgas, cassowaries, emus, and so on. The others were never still; they even climbed the coconut palms along the beach (the same beach), wasting energy, doing nothing wastefully, without progress. They had no conversation, no minds. They had broken nails. Geraldine knew about fingernails from the first time. Jim wasn't like the others, he was quiet and still.

Nights were cool but humid, hateful and sticky in a tent with insect repellent. Not the crisp cold of the nights coming up inland. Inland the cold was colder, the heat hotter. But dry, never this damp Pacific wind. Geraldine knew all about it, and how the terrain would be when they went north from Cairns. She smiled at their silly guesses and said nothing. She'd expected Jim to consult her but he hadn't, not once. Some of the others slept outside on their stretchers.

This time she'd go right to the end. Somewhere find meaning. Some meaning in life, or meaning in some one thing. Noel with his puns turning back. Giving up. We've reached the point of no return. No point, goddess, at this point in time. Dear silly Noel. Who was pointless now? Geraldine knew there had to be a goal, something other than triumph, escape, sanctuary. Something more than a justification. She felt no guilt. Felt only that it was right to be going again over the same ground. Sorting things out. Searching. Understanding why things had happened so. Armed with the first time was having second sight, giving a grip on disaster.

On a literal level, this time she was recording all physical details: soil and rocks, trees and flowers, birds and animals, the number and condition of rivers, weather changes. Such things were an aid to memory; even years later a few words could jolt back entire peopled scenes and perhaps expose motives hidden at the time. It would have been pointless last year, because Noel had his motive established months before.

The fat notebook was a comforting weight in her hand-bag. She'd missed the first two days; the blurry start of it all was to blame for that. But since then the trip had settled into the rut all things settle into, so she had about seven days' entries. Already the panic of the first two days was laughable. That was all over: bogies in this big emptiness.

Their tents were on a camping site (the same one) behind a beach. The bright blue canvas, so like orange, jarred against the lustrous greens of the big steep hill behind. With bits of washing strung from them the tents looked tattily human. The others were on the beach. Each day Geraldine hoped they'd be moving off on the next. It was three nights now they'd been here. She could have tried for a motel, even though Cairns was crowded for the season. The beach was some miles out of Cairns. She'd ask the names of trees and shrubs for the record. This tree she was under, for instance. The camping site and an Amenities Block of dirty concrete. Women one end and men the other.

'Should be moving out tomorrow.'

Geraldine hated to be crept up on. But she smiled up at Jim as he came round in front of her. 'You've said that every day.'

'They said today for the chains. I'll get my lunch while I'm in town.' He didn't ask her to go with him, just gave her a friendly salute.

Geraldine watched Jim throw his towel over the line that ran from his tent, then go to the Land-Rover they shared. He'd been for a swim with the others; they'd ask him questions about her. He'd come out of his way to speak to her. He started up, backed, and drove off.

Sometimes a sudden glimpse of Jim gave her a start, his build was so like Noel's. But that was all the resemblance. Colourful Noel who laughed and dominated. Jim was quiet and reserved, but outdoorsy, tough and capable; he liked to get on with a job and get things done. Eyes bluer with the tan, neat fairer hair. Geraldine saw him on a ship, or the land, or somewhere involving immense and quiet distance. Had he said an accountant? He'd popped up somehow into Noel's crowd during the last year, Nerida's year.

She saw one of the others returning to camp. He, or perhaps she, might or might not have seen Geraldine, in any case would ignore her. He or she hung a mirror and combed its long wet hair, shoved the comb in a pocket and set about getting lunch with dandruffy hands. There were five or six of them, Geraldine thought, and they travelled in the other three vehicles. They had names like Joey and Davey and Paulie and Willie and Chrissie. Little faces. In just a decade faces were so much smaller. They were hopeless impractical gigglers. She hadn't sorted out their sexes, and it seemed unlikely that she would. They had the same hair and voices and clothes. Some nights two of them, or at any rate more than one, got together, whispering and giggling and panting, sleazy and sexless behind a tent.

Two more drifted back. One had the shape of a female and was gobbling biscuits from a torn-open pack. The other went down on his haunches and began to chop the outside husk from an unripe coconut, using a tomahawk. The biscuit-eater nudged the food-getter with a furtive smirk towards Geraldine. It was her groundsheet that amused them; they made a big scene of roughing it among bull ants and broken roots. Jim had brought a stock of goods they'd replenish as required, but on no account alcohol, he ruled. The others stopped at wayside cafés for biscuits and chocolate, meat pies and sticky drinks. Soon they'd run out of wayside cafés.

She'd have just a milk shake for lunch at the cafe along the beach.

The others thought camp life great, but how would they react to the rough going? Jim would measure up. Jim had a dogged quality. Geraldine liked his stamina; it gave her a safe feeling. Jim wouldn't shift and change, turn back as Noel had.

All she recalled about leaving Sydney was the date and the early start. The rest was a fog. It had been cold because there'd been woollies, and she seemed to remember the wind-screens iced in the early mornings. Ten days later and it was so hot, but Cairns was nearly 2,000 kilometres north of Sydney. They'd come through small and bigger towns over a lot of flat country, but earlier they must have crossed the Blue Mountains to the plains beyond. She remembered camp-fires but only as coloured images without sound or movement. Yet some things stood out sharp in memory: white cockatoos, a wild pig, isolated houses of timber or stone or pinkish brick, a wedge-tailed eagle, Jim's first surliness. These things were in her diary. Geraldine got the fat book out and opened it. It was a shock to find only one entry, momentarily confusing to remember jotting things down and find them vanished. She read the entry:

15 JULY, 4TH DAY: Jim knows everything, names of trees like box and ironbark. The panic gone. They see nothing. I show nothing. Jim morose last night. Dinner poisonous stew. Sun all day. Bitter nights. The others a poisonous, useless bunch. Jim does any repairs.

Where was the record of terrain and weather? Geraldine shut the book. There'd been all the different greens, a spectrum of greens after rain. In places the road was as straight as a ruler. Somewhere, at some little town, there was a tiny soldier with slouch hat and rifle on an enormously high pedestal, a dusty bronze reminder of World War 1. The others were shouting, pointing, stopping because of a kangaroo. Somewhere a lot of bottle trees, somewhere they'd crossed Capricorn and the Queensland border, and somewhere they'd been held up by a road-making project, stuck for hours in mud. It was then that Jim decided to get some chains because the road men had to pull them. Red soil changing to chocolate and black, and sil-very plains with gentle undulations. Fat cattle, big trucks, sheep, big sheds, a dingo-proof net fence. Vast grassy plains, tumbleweed patches, a lot of horses. Recent rain somewhere, and after mud the dust. Mile upon mile of six-wire fence, barbed near the top. A lot of galahs. A lot of pretty trees and shrubs and bright strange flowers; delicate little trees with feathery fronds, pink and silver bottle brushes and a sort of red-hot poker in bright orange, small trees with big shiny leaves in sagey green, clumps of orange spiky flowers: details returning with the amazement she'd felt at all this living beauty in the dead outback. It had seemed to mean something and should all be recorded in the notebook.

Clouds of dust after the mud. At some small café there was a woman in bright blue plastic hair rollers in the middle of nowhere. A mangy hotel with a tiny fly-blown bar forbidden to women. She'd sat in the Land-Rover, and Jim had brought beer in cans. The others stood around in the sunlit dust guffawing at the primitive pub; drinking, giggling and knocking each other about like thoughtless puppies. Without the attractions of puppies.

'Where did you find them?' she'd asked Jim as he leaned on her door, serious face brooding at the dusty road.

'They're all right.' One of Jim's non-answers, take it or leave it.

Eastward then towards the coast and all a blank except for nice old buildings at Charters Towers, an oasis after the endless bushy road. Then suddenly on the sixth day they passed through Townsville. From now on the landscape would all go into her notebook.

But at once she forgot the notebook because Townsville brought back Noel who'd come on there alone after giving up half way between Brisbane and Cairns at some place beginning with B. Letting her find out later in Sydney that he'd slunk on after them to Townsville. So sly. Slyly sneaking behind for a plane back to Sydney. He could have come on openly with Geraldine and the others who were, after all, his responsibility, his underhand plot. Instead he'd dropped out at some place that was no distance at all and then crept after them to Townsville, dodging his guilt, just as he'd thrown in his job, then dumped Dennis for the expedition, then slid away from that in betrayal of Geraldine. Shifty Noel, never admitting the weakness she'd overlooked in ten years of marriage. Knowing she'd go on because she had to see the completion of things. Alone, nearly to the end, meaning without Noel. Until the others caved in – Don, Bernard and Julie – as people do. Time then to fly home to darling Noel and face the unexpected, shattering end: Noel with Nerida. The host of former fears falling away meaningless. Because Nerida had meaning. Foxy Nerida, small, golden and lovely.

Townsville the first time just a name because of Noel's desertion. Now there was Jim letting her see it all, terse but courteous, not a cunning plotter like Noel. Townsville now was a part of the new reality, and Geraldine would remember its big timber hotels tiered with lacy balconies and the train through the heart of it shrieking its siren. Magnetic Island off shore, and behind the city picturesque hills of bar rock, grey and pink, patched with green. A waterfall streaming like tears down the cliff face. And the lush vegetation, such crazy brilliant colours, a smell of tropics. And houses on stilts, docks and boats, fountains. Forget the sleazy shops and garish automarts, the standardised architecture of the new, because peace obliterated paltry reminders, and Jim was so nice, so strong, so dependable, such a comfort. Jim was like his talk: down-to-earth. He liked Geraldine for her level head and would never comprehend the swamping love she felt for Noel. It was just how Geraldine wanted it: cut-and-dried.

Jim would go all the way; he wasn't a man to leave things unfinished. She'd heard his sharp words when one of the others skimped a job or dropped it half done. Jim was boss and let them know it. He'd like solutions, his accountant's mind. Jim wouldn't be daunted by wild rivers and mangroves. Together they'd see it through, each sure of the other's strength.

North through Ingham, past the little sugar trams running through the cane that stretched for mile after mile. Then

Innisfail and the sunset sky so immense and lovely that Geraldine nestled close to Jim in the way Noel had loved. But Jim went sort of rigid, she remembered.

So then they got to Cairns with its hold-up, the inactivity that changed the course of thought, bringing Noel back too soon before the perspective was right.

Geraldine opened the notebook.

21 JULY, CAIRNS: I catch Jim staring. He admires my quiet fortitude. He's surly but nice, recognises quality.

Satisfied, Geraldine put the book away. On her way to the Amenities Block she saw the man again, the quiet big man with grey eyes she'd seen two days before, with the sad face.

CHAPTER 18

—————

Adrift in the long afternoon. The same people in middle years and tents with varicose veins retired collecting gemstones. Brown, healthy, unselfconscious. Polythene bags with opal, garnet, agate, sapphire, topaz, amethyst, chunks of opalised wood. Tipped out for the others crowding to see, five of them. Lounge chairs, generators, Portagas: travel in comfort. On the move two years, never constipated.

Everything the same except her objective: the purifying peace. These others were nothing, the meals and the heat nothing. Intellect and experience effecting the victory. The first time, after Noel's desertion, there'd been moments of weakness. At times she'd thought the exhaustion, the dirt and humid orange nights, the monotonous landscape that only in retrospect showed its rich variety, must be run from as Noel had run from her. At times in the orange tent she'd looked back on their city life as enchanting and thought herself mad in not returning with Noel. Only strong will kept her going forward, and curiosity over Noel's motive. His real motive, not those lying excuses. She'd thought by going on she'd reach the truth. There'd been troubling questions. Would her absence matter? Would it even be noticed? Would she drop from the scene as someone dead? Would the city go on without her? And her house, the oasis of peace that was really only the peace of her restraint with Noel, would that continue? Or would the void be filled with substance, with flesh and touching, and would laughter and talk rush in to fill her silence? Each mile covered she'd thought a victory, each fresh question a new source of strength. And got her dusty answer.

A bearded Aborigine lighting his fire with sticks. A brown old spinster in a print dress and self-sufficiency.

Choke back the tears. Once started it would be for everything. And then it would be over. But not yet.

'Woman had quads there last week, doubled the population.' A scream of harsh laughter.

They measure rainfall in feet, not inches.

So clear they were: Noel and Nerida dead, together. Did anyone tell her how they died? If there were wounds they'd kept them secret. Just this image of two naked bodies on a slab, side by side, touching, overlapping.

The same storm clouds all day long on the sea's edge.

I never want to see a tent again.

'Hey, Gerry, Jim's back with the gear.'

Geraldine stared. 'My name is Geraldine.'

The young person with dancing dirty hair edged back, looking uncertain. Then turned and ran.

Some time later Jim's voice was neutral. 'Miles away,' he said. 'Dinner's nearly ready; we leave in the morning. I suggest an early night.' It was a relief that Jim never touched her.

Walking back with him to the fire and good smell. He'd got steak in Cairns. The others there, hungry. She counted five. Why did she have six fixed in her head? Well, if one were lost or strayed that was all to the good.

Geraldine slept for almost nine hours. It was the mood of expectancy, the end of stagnation.

They got going around seven. Always first to be organised, Geraldine waited while they struck camp. She didn't help in the general work because they didn't appreciate her help. Jim did her share as a matter of course. How silly they were with their horseplay. Thank heaven for Jim. Jim was the only one she could tolerate, the only one to acknowledge her wishes and wants. All she'd noticed of him in their few encounters were his blue eyes and the quiet manner so foreign to Noel's crowd. Now she'd seen his inner strength, a stamina like her own, such a necessary quality to cope with the harshness that lay ahead.

The same muddle of departure.

'Ready?' someone asked. It was right in her ear and a hand touched her.

Geraldine looked up into the silly young face. 'Don't do that, not *ever*.'

His mouth fell open. 'Bloody maniac!' He stamped off.

Nobody since Noel. Right up to the time he became Nerida's Noel. Touching Nerida.

'We're off now, Geraldine,' Jim said.

A relief to be on the move again, shut in with Jim's compassionate understanding. The initial splendid scenery, the road winding along the coast between hills and the turquoise island-dotted sea. She remembered Don's thirteen rivers to cross and smiled, knowing the hundreds of creeks that were tougher barriers. Among the sugar three motor-bikes roared round them from behind. The pointed black peaks closed in on the left. A small Land-Rover overtook them just before the Mount Molloy turn-off. There were the Gorge and the Devil's Thumb, like old friends.

Geraldine scarcely needed the map that was open on her knees. She knew where the choking red dust began, where the hill humidity made torrents of sweat down all the body's gullies.

'Did you expect the road as bad as this?' she asked Jim.

'She gets worse later,' he said.

But he knew only from information, not from experience. One had to experience to know. Jim drove well with a calm face, not with Noel's frowning erratic spurts or Don's witty obscenities. Jim was silent and that was restful.

They lunched without shade at the side of the red road. They piddled in dust and privacy behind their Land-Rovers. Later they'd be laxer. Geraldine saw the small Land-Rover stationary ahead of them. The man moving around it looked somehow familiar. She sat inside with her sandwiches and listened to idiot theories on snakes and scorpions. She thought of the dead taipan. Real snakes were more to be trusted than the other kind.

During the afternoon Jim asked, 'You all right?'

'I'm fine,' Geraldine said.

They passed a derelict car, then another, and soon after that the small Land-Rover. Red with dust, it was pulled up on the roadside. The driver was writing something.

Then flatter country and the scrub, the remembered desolation. Just about here Don had turned off the road for the night.

'Very soon now there's a nice spot to camp on the Laura River,' Geraldine said.

Jim grunted, then a minute later said, 'I've had it for today,' and at once turned off the road into identical bush.

Resentment rose. 'Why here?'

Jim got out and bent his head to look at her. 'I've got it all mapped out, thanks all the same.'

He began thrashing about as Don had. There was every excuse for Don on an unknown road, but Jim had her experience he'd professed to be so keen about.

Waiting depressed in the Land-Rover she got out her notebook.

22 JULY: Jim is being stupidly perverse.

The others arrived in high spirits. Four vehicles made a crowd on the side of the road in the tangle of scrub. They had a fire going in minutes. Jim said no tents, sleep on stretchers in the open.

'I'll put yours up,' he said to Geraldine and got busy on it at once.

Geraldine made no reply. He mind had jerked into low gear. Soon chops were sizzling and spluttering and sparks flying up into the dry branches overhead. How like them to start a bushfire. Jim watched uncaring, his face morose. The change in Jim was mystifying. Vinnie or Paulie made an obscene gesture at her tent and the others rolled about laughing. Throughout the meal they whispered and giggled tiresomely. Jim brooded on some inner thing. Geraldine didn't wait for coffee because the atmosphere, in some curious way, held a worse tension than that of last year's open sniping. Feeling eyes on her back she began preparations for her scrappy bath. This caused new paroxysms among the others.

Ready for bed she said a pleasant good night. One voice replied from round the dying fire but it wasn't Jim's.

Blue canvas, a blue night. A fine night, a half moon. Blue canvas glowing suddenly orange and stealthy movements close outside. Geraldine held her breath. Was it one of them with a torch on the way to bed? Was it as innocent as that?

She wakened many times during the night, alert and straining, hearing in the familiar sounds of the bush something inimical, a threatening something that terrified her because it was inexplicable. Crackles and splinterings of an unknown kind.

But the morning was prosaic with giggles, birdsong and muddle. Jim's face was back in place. The early air was good to breathe. Soon they were on their way.

'Did you sleep well?' Geraldine's voice polite as she settled into her place.

'Like a log,' Jim said.

The man in the small Land-Rover passed by as Jim came out on the road. Geraldine recognised him. This was the third time she'd seen him. She'd seen him twice at Cairns with his sad face and grey eyes. He looked too big for the driver's seat, big hands. He must have camped in the same kind of desolate bush. He was moving about the rate they did and in the same direction.

They passed the pleasant spot on the Laura River, but Jim said nothing. The others kept shouting to stop; it seemed they were mad about birds suddenly. Jim waved them on, sure of their obedience.

'Quite a few mossies around last night,' Jim said. He'd seen her scratching. Geraldine had smeared on insect repellent and wondered now whether it was her stupid alarm in the night that had attracted the mosquitoes.

Just before Road Junction they passed the three bikies who'd whizzed round them on the coast road yesterday. The bikies shouted and grinned and waved their beer bottles. Geraldine saw the small Land-Rover in the distance outside the hotel.

Jim pulled in behind it. 'Too early for a beer?' he asked.

'I'd love one.'

He came round and held her door and gave her the smile from Sydney. He'd been tired yesterday, she guessed, with the strain of organisation. The others roared up in clouds of dust.

She followed Jim to one end of the bar. The youngsters massed in the middle, an explosion of noise that threw the silence at each end into sharp relief. The matching quiet was the big man from the small Land-Rover. Just these few glimpses, merging paths that never meet, like the bikie youths.

Jim drank his beer fast and said he'd be back for another; he'd just duck into the store for bread and stuff. Without looking, Geraldine was aware of the big man leaving, but almost in the same instant found he was beside her.

'Morning,' he said.

'Good morning.'

'Going far?'

'Up to the top.'

'How're you enjoying it?'

'Very much,' Geraldine said smiling, 'I'm keeping a record of everything, landscape, birds, every detail.'

'Good idea.' He threw a small nod at the others. 'Where do the kids fit in?'

'You mean I don't.' The man smiled back but his eyes remained sad. 'They're friends of our leader, the man who organised it all.'

Geraldine could see he liked her. He'd be in his forties, she thought. The grey eyes were pale; he was big and muscular with enormous hands, nondescript hair. But he had repose that went with his face. She noticed these things while their uninspired chatting continued. Pointless talk about tents and meals and distances. What made her think of a newsprint detective? That's what he looked like, one of those smudgy blobs inset beside a picture of a house with a cross on a window. But he wasn't smudgy, just pale and settled with sadness. Not a scrap like the real ones who'd been so silly and tiresome in Sydney. She remembered one name, Wells, because of water. A woolly feeling shut her off, and she exchanged inanities with this stodgy man who was perhaps a recent widower.

'You're from Sydney?' he asked.

'Yes, Woollahra.'

'My home's in Westmead,' he said. 'Two kids. I'm just getting used to my wife leaving me.'

'And this is a holiday?'

'I've got the sort of job takes me about a bit.'

Jim came back. 'My name's Turner,' the man said. Jim said he was Jim Oates.

'Yes, I know Woollahra well,' Turner said.

Dreamily while they drank more beer Geraldine saw this man passing by, perhaps even seeing, the very place where Noel and Nerida had died.

'My name's Geraldine,' she said suddenly.

'Nice.' He smiled.

She didn't tell him Blaine; he didn't ask. But this man liked her, he was interested. He didn't want her to be a passing ship. She liked the way he watched her, liked his eyes on her.

'Ready?' Jim said.

'Might bump into you again,' Turner said with a smile as they left.

―――

CHAPTER 19

Jim was silent all the way to Laura. They both wore sun-glasses. Jim had a vertical furrow between his eyebrows. Three times Geraldine belched from the beer.

She rested her eyes on the big earth-red stones along the sides of the road. The dust in her eyes and throat was the same colour. She expected gentleness from Jim, a constant concern; his air of quiet chivalry was the only clear-cut memory she had from their few vague meetings in Sydney. The road changed abruptly from red to white. She saw Jim picking the hard red dust from his nose and flicking it out of the Land-Rover. A sign saying Detour pointed into thick scrub. The iron telegraph poles. Eternity on a post. The landscape and its details were cosily familiar as something kept from childhood, but Geraldine would not let sentimentality obscure her purpose. Behind the surface lay pitfalls of barren-ness and anger, of lost directions and human frailty. It was a hard road as it had been with Noel. She'd exposed the base-ness under his bland exterior.

'You're getting out?'

They'd stopped outside the pub at Laura. Jim's head was turned to her. She didn't like his sunglasses. They were too black. Face to face with him she couldn't tell where his eyes were. They might be beyond her or they might not.

'Isn't it time for lunch?'

'Yep.' He got out and slammed his door.

She saw him go into the pub. She waited until the others followed like a lot of sheep. She got out then and went into the adjacent store. The few customers were Aborigines and one white man. A busy, worn-looking woman bustling behind the counter threw her a look and a smile. Geraldine waited her turn and smiled at two black children sucking things on sticks and staring at her with solemn eyes.

'Yes, love?' the woman said.

'Do you serve tea?'

'I can give you a cup. It's always on the go.' The woman ducked through the open door behind her and Geraldine watched her lift a great stained enamel teapot from the stove with one hand, pick up one of several turned-down plastic mugs and pour.

'Milk and sugar, love?' she called.

'Just milk, please.'

The woman brought the mug of tea and said, 'Something to eat, dear? We don't really do this, but as I've got it going and I expect you're hungry.'

'I'd love a sandwich if you can manage it.'

'Corned beef do?'

'Fine.'

The doorstep sandwich was wonderful, white plastic lathered with mustard. And so were the shelves from ceiling to floor chock-a-block with provisions. Between and over them hung boots, sandshoes, rubber thongs, kettles, billy cans, whips, belts and riding-boots, and bowls of tin and plastic. Drums and kegs and rolls of netting stood about on the floor. There was dust over everything and the woman, who looked clean if untidy, must have a dreadful time keeping a neck ahead.

While she was drinking her second mug of tea Jim stalked in with his dead black circles of eyes and started selecting stores. Instant coffee, packets of tea, corned beef, soya beans. Jim had surprised her with his Yep. It had implied an insult.

The woman told her where the loo was. A leaning shed at

the end of the back yard. On its door the legend, '4U2P'. The woman let her wash her hands at the sink.

Geraldine went outside to wait. The others were there in a knot of laughter and shouts. They'd met an Aboriginal man in the pub.

'Talks real good,' Vinnie or Vickie said. 'Talks as good as us.'

Two men Geraldine had seen at the Cairns beach drove up in an old open car. They were laden with gear. They looked fiftyish.

Jim called from the door of the store for the others to lend a hand. While the supplies were being stowed Willie or someone said to Jim, 'Don't panic if we lag a bit. Bloody dust's like a mushroom cloud at the back, just rises and hangs in the bloody air.'

'Okay,' Jim said.

While the tanks were being filled Geraldine sat on the wooden bench outside the pub and got out her notebook. She had the date on her watch.

23 JULY: Jim less considerate.

She stared at the road, then, remembering, added, *Dust*.

Just as they were pulling out Jim saluted somebody with a smile. Geraldine saw that it was the small Land-Rover. Then they were into the dust again and the huge anthills stuck in the low scrub. She'd tried to tell Noel about them but he hadn't been interested. Around 150 kilometres to Musgrave where the tree was full of galahs. Geraldine knew they'd see the big man again, and also the older men in the old open car. As for the bikies in T-shirts, they might be the same ones from last year roaring up and down the Peninsula all year long. It was a small world in such empty distances.

They stopped at the Hann River and paddled in the shallow water as they had last year. It was wide even in the dry season. The young ones got into togs and plunged right in. Jim stood in the water watching them. Geraldine stayed on the bank. She wore light canvas shoes. She knew what to bring from the first time. The others were told boots and in the heat resorted to bare feet. Jim only had to ask. She knew what clothes, and about lots of soap and lavatory rolls, and tissues and a plastic bowl to wash in and the indispensable insect repellent.

They camped early by the river bed at Musgrave. It was almost dry. The big house was up the rise, and Geraldine could see the small tree. It looked bare. A light plane was on the airstrip. The hot still afternoon air, where they'd stopped in a dip under big trees, was full of tiny flying things in clouds. Chrissie or someone came hurtling back with a snake alarm. It turned out to be a grey fallen log. Geraldine knew how elusive snakes were, timid things unless obstructed, far gentler than people.

An argument started during dinner over the share of work. Geraldine stayed calmly out of it. She'd known there'd be rows. It had been the same with Don, Bernard and Julie. It was expected on safari, perhaps to show the small measure of human endurance. When the shouting died down she heard Jim's voice, quiet and authoritative.

A sort of sulky peace came, and some of them started putting up the tents. She sat apart with her coffee. An engine rumbled into the silent dusk and the small Land-Rover descended the slope and pulled up about 50 metres away. The big man got out, stretched, then started strolling towards them. Jim stood up.

He looked down at Geraldine and said, 'You might give the others a hand,' then moved to meet the man named Turner.

Geraldine didn't budge. She watched Jim and Turner talking. What did they have to talk about? They looked serious and engrossed in the half dark. Men were like that, cloaking trivialities with an air of importance and intrigue, putting on faces of grave concern over some dull interchange about mud and dust.

The washing-up was done, excluding Geraldine's, which she preferred to do herself. The tents were almost ready. Today the others had shown the first cracks in their happy-go-lucky veneer. She'd waited for the signs. She would never participate in silly flare-ups and the sulking that always followed. Calm and controlled. A rational manner and reasoned reactions. Even when she saw Chrissie or Willie washing its feet in the washing-up bowl her rebuke, though sharp, was gentle.

'Stop that – it's filthy!'

The young person stared rudely and said, 'You're nuts,' then lit a cigarette and went on with its brazen stare and its feet in the bowl.

Geraldine wisely turned her back.

Jim returned then bringing Turner, looking shy, with him. Turner nodded and smiled at Geraldine. Jim said no more along the lines of giving a hand. He'd wanted to exert authority, and having already subdued the others he'd picked on Geraldine. It was only the rumblings of discontent compounding his fatigue. Jim knew she was out of a different box and most of the time treated her accordingly.

Turner was on the other side of the fire exchanging talk with the kids, who were relaxed now, their work done. Feet were still in the washing-up bowl. Turner didn't say much; he drew them out with brief questions and his encouraging smile. A silent solitary man. A man with a load of trouble. Had he loved his deserting wife so much? The weight he carried seemed greater than that. She'd thought he was a newsprint picture of a detective, but watching him now she put him down as a small businessman overpowered by giants. In any case it didn't matter. The way when they ran into him his eyes sought her out, focused on her at once. The usual bewitchment. She cared nothing, all that was over. He was just another traveller looking for peace of a kind, another wanderer in small circles seeking some point out of the round-about. The fiftyish men and the bikie youths too, all searching for a reason.

Turner left them then to cook his meal. Jim seemed set to outsit everybody, brooding into the fire and now and again throwing little useless twigs in. He seemed not to hear as the others, one by one, said goodnight. Soon it was just Geraldine and Jim and the fire. Jim was really being quite strange. She hadn't expected displays of temperament. She watched the slow methodical movements of Turner in the distance and wished it was he in charge of their trip.

Geraldine got up. She smiled down at Jim.

'This lethargy,' she said, 'it'll take every ounce of energy to make me wash tonight.'

Jim didn't smile or look up. 'I mean it about pulling your weight,' he said, 'you're a strong healthy woman.'

Anger stirred in Geraldine. 'The trip's getting you down; it's harder than you thought.'

'It's a good life,' Jim said.

'Perhaps you're sleeping badly. Don't take it out on me.' She moved towards her tent but this quiet voice followed.

'Justice is all I want.'

Geraldine shut her ears and went on into her tent. She wouldn't be drawn into their petty nigglings. Justice was a big word for camp chores. It was a surprise and was best countered by ignoring it. When she took her bowl outside to get some hot water from the big black kettle by the fire Jim was still there, still brooding. He didn't speak or look at her.

Soon she was in bed, washed and scented. Noel's cuddly kitten. There was nobody now to snuggle up to. She could hear the rhythmic groan of stretchers. They seemed to be always at it. Some nights they were worse than the mosquitoes. She didn't believe Jim found it easy to sleep. Some mornings, before he put on his round black opaque glasses, his blue eyes were dark-rimmed and sunken and new grim lines showed round his mouth.

She wondered whether Turner was asleep. Paths cross: a junction that may end there – or begin a convergence. Events and people meet and dash, explode and part again and vanish, or become embroiled. No matter. No more mood of expectancy. Noel was gone and she was adrift on a fuzzy plane between buoyancy and despair, feeling nothing.

People like Noel don't grow up, they just get older. There were no people like Noel.

Nothing was stirring. The tangled bush. The stars close, so many through the little net square, stars never seen in the city. She could reach out and touch them.

She caught her breath. A movement. A soft rustling. She lay still. There were sounds after all. Things do stir; the bush is always awake with stealthy whispers and little snaps. A movement of a different kind. Close to her tent. Too close. A shadow on the blue canvas, a glow of orange. Jim going to bed at last? Or some other shape, unidentifiable?

The blur was Noel's fault. Darling thoughtless Noel. But Noel was gone and the agony with him. Strange that the second parting had no poignancy, so unlike the desolation of the first. She felt nothing. Pathetic old puns. Why had she taken them to heart so? Little things can eat away. Noel had said that of her fussing. She'd smothered him. Pinioned: another word he'd used. Everlasting supervision and jealousy. Noel had said it was irritating beyond endurance, just before he'd turned back. It was her love he'd given such trivial labels. Loving was a very different thing from punning. And all excuses because he'd planned to go back. Noel intended everything behind that lying smile. He'd brought his slipperiness right out into the open. Fussing: strange how that silly word could still stir resentment. How understanding she'd been, how tolerant, and he'd gone out of his way to upset her just so he could accuse her of having one of her turns. Her turns were his concoction, just to use against her. Where had Noel dropped out? It had been a sad place.

Geraldine's stretcher creaked in the bright blue tent.

I'm safe now.

She thought of the lonely man Turner and shivered in the humidity.

I'm lonely too, my life like his will be lonely from now on.

A sob constricted her throat.

But I'm safe now.

She was absolutely safe. The police had lost interest, just two accidental deaths, and the old crowd had all drifted back to their own lives. She'd stood at a distance, uninvolved, yet knowing what was happening. The only link was Jim, and that so tenuous it counted for nothing. On the edge of the crowd, and only a few times. It was a surprise he'd cropped up at all because plainly he didn't fit in with Noel's set. A friend of a friend of a friend.

Was he still out there staring into the dying fire? The tents were close together on the river bed. She was afraid to go and look. It was a new feeling, to be afraid of the dark. Of unseen rustling. She didn't have to leave her tent; she had a plastic bucket for peeing. But the tingle of fear stayed.

She knew the others talked about her. They laughed at her behind their hands like children, encouraged each other with silly gestures and faces. When the crack-up started they'd begin plotting against her. It was they who'd got Jim to tell her to do her share. He'd hated saying it, and this accounted for his odd manner and moody fire-watching. It was foreign to Jim to be terse and unkind and it was this that worried him.

Then suddenly the truth hit: Jim was in love with her.

The stretcher groaned and wheezed as she sat up and groped for her bag. She felt for the notebook, switched on her torch and got out her pen.

23 JULY, NIGHT: Jim is in love with me. It explains everything. Even in Sydney, asking me to join the trip. It makes him uncomfortable, knowing my grief for Noel. Poor Jim.

It was satisfying to solve the only little conundrum. The incredible thing was it not occurring before. So many precedents like Clyde, Dennis, Andrew. She settled down on the noisy stretcher and was asleep almost at once.

————

CHAPTER 20

Geraldine was up first. It was five-thirty. She washed her hands and face in cold water. There was still a faint glow under the ashes and the fire was easy to rekindle with dry sticks that lay about plentifully. Shreds of dead bark made a blaze in no time and then she piled on larger pieces of wood the others had collected yesterday under Jim's orders. She didn't look his way but was aware of Turner up and about. She filled the two big billy cans and the black kettle and got them all going on the fire. If Noel could see her he wouldn't believe his eyes.

The others emerged singly, grateful for breakfasty sounds, smirking when they saw who was responsible. Only Jim had no expression, his face weary and blank. He said to step on it. He was anxious to be on the road again.

They left before seven. Packing was careless and quick. Jim's mind seemed far away. Soon they were into the enormous grey anthills and spindly trees, on the road of snowy sand that Geraldine remembered thinking was like headache powders. Even above their engine she would hear shrieks of oohs and aahs from the others. They'd want a few halts; they wouldn't like Jim's gruelling non-stop drive. Only Geraldine was glad of it. She stole a look at his set face that only saw the road ahead, without pleasure or anticipation. It dawned on her that she didn't know him at all. He might have some other great sorrow, perhaps a terminal illness. Or he might be the kind of pessimist whose gloomy view nothing could shift. A pity he wasn't like Turner, a man reconciled to life's vicissitudes. There's been no conversing with Turner this morning, just a distant wave when they left.

The little palms with feathery tops, the trees thicker, the deep sand slowing driving, then a dustier, coarser road, thick red dust and the sun beating in on them.

'Jesus!' Jim muttered. It might be the flies that stuck to his face, or the heat made worse by the flies, or the endless dusty road ahead made worse by the heat and the flies. Or the bumps and ruts in the road disguised in their blanket of dust. Then he said, 'You okay?'

'I'm fine. Remember, I've done it before.'

Jim grunted.

Geraldine wasn't at all fine. Her briefs, cotton for absorbency, were stuck in the sweat of her shut thighs. Pain was trampling her left shoulder and creeping across the back of her neck. The big breasts Noel had loved (he'd said) were a sticky unbearable weight. She'd got, incredibly, fatter, more solid. Despite sunglasses, her eyes stung with glare and with staring at the road. Dust was in her nostrils, ears and hair and with the sweat formed a glue that was pasted all over her. The pain wouldn't last; it was only the sitting all day. She hated doctors. They knew nothing: a doctor would say it was tension and nerves and toss in a few more synonyms for good measure.

My feet ache.

She took her shoes off and glanced at Jim's big hard implacable boots.

My feet stink.

They passed the two men in their fifties and old car, stopped by the roadside. Had they got in front during the night? One had a reddish face; the other was thin and looked near death. They had a Thermos flask.

'It was the same last year,' Geraldine said. 'The same people over and over.'

Jim made no reply. Why did she bother? Where was the yearning tenderness she expected? His unfriendliness was puzzling. It was also tiresome and stupid in circumstances that threw them together day after day. There was an unavoidable intimacy for two people on a long rough road, shut in side by side for endless hours. They got to know things about each other. They got to know about coughs and bowels and bladders, about fortitude and purpose, about twitches and body odours, teeth and halitosis, lies and evasions.

Jim had noticed the two men. He'd noticed the bikies too. She knew Jim was observant: another thing proximity revealed. He'd noticed Turner even at Cairns, just as Turner was equally aware of them. Of course, Turner singled her out for particular attention, but that was to be expected.

The same road seemed to go on for ever but Geraldine knew that it didn't. Monotony was full of little shocks. Like the wide shallow river suddenly that she'd forgotten, trickling over stones. Soon they'd be at Coen.

Jim pulled up. 'We'll have lunch here.' He got out and slammed his door.

Three of the others splashed in naked, then came back for soap. Geraldine took her swimsuit into the trees and changed there. She bathed apart from the others, soaping herself all over. The water was only knee-deep but clear and flowing. They'd never know what a swimmer she was.

After drying herself she went to their Land-Rover and fished out clean clothes. A coat of red dust was on everything. The others splashed and giggled near the bank. Jim was getting lunch. He hadn't been in the water. Geraldine got out deodorant, talcum and three pairs of briefs to wash. She could feel eyes on her body. It was her big womanly breasts that drew the hated looks. She threw the towel round her shoulders.

'Who's she think she is?' a voice said.

'Who cares?' another answered, 'I wouldn't waste any time on that big broad.'

Geraldine burned with hatred. She took her things back to
the trees, making herself saunter. Jim would have heard. She
expected him to put them in their place, curb if not cure their
rudeness. He must have heard a lot of their disparagement
since the trip began. She balanced on stones in the running
water and washed out the pants. Then she took them back
and spread them on her seat in the Land-Rover.

Lunch was slices of Devon sausage with tomato sauce and
sliced plastic bread. Geraldine had two dry Ryvitas from her
tin. The others were nearly nude, refreshed by the dip, full of
wisecracks and silly laughter. They looked clean and almost
human. They begged for another quick dip.

'Okay,' Jim said, 'but make it snappy.'

Geraldine washed the things in the river and dried them
on paper towels. Soon they'd be out of paper towels. She sat
down beside Jim.

'Aren't you having a dip?' she asked kindly.

'No.'

'It would help you through the afternoon.'

'I don't like water in bulk.'

'Volume,' Geraldine said. But the corrective wit fell flat
as it had with Noel. She was silent then and watched the
youngsters with him. Something recurred to her. 'Weren't
there to be six? I seem to remember six besides you and
me.'

'Yes.' No sound could be terser.

'Somebody dropped out?'

'Yes, My girl.'

'Oh.' She hadn't thought of Jim in relation to a girl. He'd
seemed solitary. What should she say? Anything at all?
Something light? 'Not a bust-up, I hope?'

'She died.'

'Oh, I'm sorry.' Geraldine felt sad because it brought Noel
back. How strange that Jim had suffered the same loss. It
threw yet another light on his moody manner. Clearly he'd
taken it very hard. She wanted to say something about Noel

that would bring them closer together, but she found no words and said nothing.

Late in the afternoon, roused from torpor by an enormous jolt, beyond Coen where they'd stopped briefly to replenish perishables, Geraldine said in a sleepy voice, 'I'm terribly sorry about your girl.'

Jim remained silent. She looked at him sideways. His face was scrunched-up with grief. Should she pursue it, feeling so headachey? It would be nice to clear the air before the headache set in.

'What was her name?' she asked, her voice gentle.

'What's the difference?'

For some reason Nerida entered her head. Absurd, of course, but it didn't stop the queerest sensation in her chest, like ice, a lump of ice. And then a panicky pounding. It was because of water and Jim so grim and herself drowsy. Of course not Nerida, Jim would have said something.

Jim hadn't moved; his face hadn't changed. Poor Jim, brooding on the sudden emptiness in his life.

She was wide awake now, and everything whirred through her head again. It was having Nerida alive in the back of her mind. The atmosphere in the Land-Rover felt electric. But that was silly, her imagination. What had she to do with Nerida's death?

Poor Jim. There was only love. What else counted, what else mattered? Wasn't that the point she'd sought with Noel? They'd each suffered a loss, she and Jim; it was something to share, to build a deep friendship upon. And making Jim's anguish worse was the guilt of his love for Geraldine that he must suppress because conscience told him he was betraying his dead girl.

Mango trees dotted about, all in flower again. Crossroads. Soon they'd come to the Archer River tumbling among its spotted rocks. Big bloody boulders, Don had called them. It was too good a place not to pitch their tents, and the time was nearly right to call it a day.

Jim had organised this trip. Happy then, untouched by tragedy, he'd got the idea after hearing Noel's highly coloured account of the first one. Geraldine had met Jim Oates a couple of times, once at Noel's Den, perhaps, and perhaps another time in somebody's garden at some poisonous Sunday lunch party; maybe had met his girl. Had he been at her house once or twice with Noel's crowd? A fish out of water among Noel's loud egotistical friends, lacking in their push. Of course he'd fallen in love with her from the first, girl or no girl, love of the kind content to worship from a distance. He never called her Gerry and never touched her; she liked that. And he was discerning, with a quality that matched her own, because he'd gone to a lot of trouble over this trip, she was certain now, simply to relieve her grief. Jim came good just when she needed sanctuary. He'd popped up in the last year, as Nerida had. Noel was always collecting people to fill in his own blanks. Nerida and Jim were only two of the new lot Noel had netted. Until the tragedy the trip was just a sometime idea to Jim. He was too cautious not to take Noel's embroideries with a pinch of salt and do his own researches. She believed now that he'd precipitated the starting time solely on her behalf. Aware of her suffering, distressed by it, with the group of kids he had, six counting his girl. Her death provided another motive for the trip: to bury his personal sorrow in its hardships.

He looked so sad, so tired yet so taut, beside her, hands clenched on the wheel. What was he thinking? Perhaps only how to mitigate each jolt on the uneven dirt road.

Jim was the only one she called by name because his face was the only one with meaning. The others were hair and legs and boots and shouts and giggles, of all sexes, unwashed and whispering, five of them, but seeming more when she wanted to be alone, and solitude in the great emptiness was hard to find. They'd been ready to start at any time; no responsibilities, or if they had, eager to cop out of them. So Jim had come to her rescue just when she needed to regain perspective. At a loose end with Noel gone. Beguiled by the Peninsula again because it was the farthest point away from further questioning. At the time it seemed Jim had played right into her hands.

So bursting out with his dead girl Jim had seemed to cloud things, raising a question mark over the trip. But now she'd fitted it in. It was her reasoning power, this ability to think things through, that showed her the sequence of events, of actions and their motives, in totality.

They'd stopped.

'It's the Archer,' she told Jim with a smile. 'I've been longing for you to see it. You can relax now.'

Jim said nothing. He got out with a door slam.

Should she call on the reserves of patience Noel had disregarded when Jim seemed bent on being as churlish as Noel?

It was the last of daylight with a full moon rising over trees. Two of the vehicles were stuck in the river sand. Jim said leave it till morning. They were on a flat area which in the summer wet would be metres under rushing water. The river just here was like a pond, but moving, and Geraldine could hear turbulence over rocks.

Jim got dinner, hard-boiled eggs with sauerkraut out of tins. He said they'd do better tomorrow. Paulie or someone said the eggs were meant for lunch. Jim said they were meant for eating, so eat them. Everyone was too dead beat for argument. The stretchers were put up in the open. The sky was clear of everything but a million stars and the big full moon, and this light mingled with that of the campfire made magic of trees and sand and water and the spotted outcrops of rock. Jim said they'd maybe stay two or three nights, find a good spot in the morning to pitch their tents. He grunted good night then and went to the row of stretchers, and the creaks and groans he made echoed round the hollow they were in.

Geraldine's stretcher was separate, erected by Jim at her request on the far side of their Land-Rover. She listened to the river and the bush and felt her spine tingle. Where was the serenity that came from understanding? Instead a sense of unease crept in and lingered. The hot blue canvas suffocated. Tangibles had her in their grip: itches; the sheet it was too hot with and too cool without; a sniffly nose; the headache still; things buzzing. And something worse, a slithery unspecified fear. Then shockingly the realisation that she was in the open and it wasn't the blue canvas that suffocated.

Daylight woke her, and laughter and raucous shouts, and the dew drenching her. She got up sneezing. They were starting on breakfast. Geraldine had a quick dip in the river, then went for a jog-trot over the river flats. It stopped the sneezing and cleared her head.

Sausages and eggs and squalour round the campfire. They looked like a nasty accident. Two sausages were left for her, cooling in a sea of fat in the big iron frying pan, put aside on the sand among eager flies. A carton of eggs was open. One or two of them were still munching on fried bread. Vinnie was wiping up egg with a finger.

'Lovely,' Geraldine said. She picked up the heavy frying pan with one hand and put it on the fire. When it started to sizzle she broke in an egg one-handed.

It might have been Willie who said, 'Gosh, that's bloody clever, I saw someone once do that on the TV.'

'I didn't know you could cook,' a girl said.

'I'm a gourmet cook,' Geraldine said with a smile.

'Been keeping it dark, haven't you?'

'I didn't come to cook.' Geraldine kept her smile as she dished up her breakfast.

'What d'you come as?'

'Adviser.' She tilted her smile at Jim, but Jim was staring off into the trees.

Sausages and eggs bought Noel back, and Julie. It seemed a long time ago and trivial, last year's search for a new beginning. The problems then had all been clear, and she'd thought soluble. It was uncanny to find new problems arisen, their nature a mystery.

Jim stood up. 'Soon as you've all finished we'll pull those vehicles out of the sand and make camp somewhere. Over there looks good.' He was looking across the pond of river at a dry sandy area that was fairly extensive. 'We're dead in the river bed here. I'll go and scout around to see if there's some way across for the Rovers.'

'Can I come?' someone asked.

'All come if you like. Mrs Blaine can wash up.'

Deaf to their going she knew when they were gone. The coarseness, the dismissal. The menial role so rudely assigned. The sneering 'Mrs Blaine'. The shock was so total it was hard to comprehend. Deep inside a burgeoning hatred mixed with the egg and sausages. She got up and left the squalid mess. It was theirs; they could clean it up.

She followed the sandy river bed. She wanted the bush to soothe her. She wished to be quiet and lonely as the morning and be restored by it. There were woodchoppers chopping wood. Sunlight filtering down. Logs and bark caught high in the trees from the last flooding rains. Heat lay in the wide river valley, the sun beat up from the earth. A scrub fowl ran along the bank and disappeared.

Perhaps she'd been wrong to expect more of Jim Oates. His reserve had fooled her into thinking him superior. Always this search for the ideal to match her own qualities.

Great stretches of sandy bed, the remaining pools drying up. A hot rank smell of rotting vegetation. The river a thin ribbon on the other side. Paperbarks, unknown trees bearing nuts, hundreds of different kinds of eucalypt. Almost quicksand between pools. River flotsam: twigs, leaves, stones, sea-weedy stuff, manure, small logs, feathers, small bones. A horse's hoof prints startlingly viridian. Lorikeets shrieking overhead, an eagle swooping after prey.

Wasn't it more than likely Jim was just like the rest of Noel's coterie?

A dead kangaroo at the base of the right bank, half eaten, perhaps by dingoes. The stillness.

She'd seen them close and becoming closer, drawn together by suffering. Now Jim was changing under her eyes. And watching her, because, for all his contemptuous rudeness, he knew every move she made. Instead of feeling free she had the sensation of being in a trap. What could be more absurd, more unexpected?

Flashes of colour among the trees drew Geraldine to the bank. She fought her way up a short distance and waited. Insects buzzing, creaks, slithers, twigs snapping, the busy birds – all the breathless silence, her own presence exploding it. A bag of leaves woven together hung from a branch, fat with some spider's or ant's secret. High above, flood drapery in the trees. Twisted trunks, sculptural shapes. Everywhere the granite boulders and outcrops spotted with glinting quartz. The sun stronger, hotter. Birds squawking, perhaps in some territorial wrangle, a woodchopper chairing their meeting.

The change in Jim. It brought to mind the change in Noel, the tense and anxious look Noel got at times. Noel's was conscience. What could make Jim so edgy? People faltered, but why Jim, who was so tough and so at home in this tough outdoor life? He coped with every problem. Was it the others getting on his nerves? Geraldine was no trouble, she never complained. Jim had said, 'Be good to have you along, someone who keeps their head.' That had been before the tragedy of deaths, but she was still the same, unaffected by death that happened all over the place. No worry there. Enquiries were ended, and people understood her wish to get away from the distressing scene. In death they looked horrible. Death was ugly, light extinguished.

Rainbow birds diving to the water after insects. Robins. The eagle again, down to the dead kangaroo. Caterpillars, ants, spiders. Great bumble-bees.

A sense of his own shortcomings might explain Jim's grudge. Was it possible he wasn't, after all, in love with her? She wouldn't be unbalanced by his antagonism. It was Noel all over again: the long haul, the immensity, exposing the basic nothing.

Harsh cries of crows. A non-stop buzzing in the silence. Tiny black birds turning out their pockets.

But why did he strain forward as if to some fixed appointment?

Geraldine returned to the river bed. Doves, white cockatoos, pigeons. She sat on a flat rock and got out her notebook and pen.

25 JULY: Jim sulky and rude. Like Noel, no real stamina. It may be his desire for me that makes him surly.

She put the things away and sat on for a while watching lizards slipping over the flat embedded rocks. Excruciating humidity enveloped her.

When she got back they were all on the other side, busy erecting the tents and chopping wood. The breakfast scene had vanished. Only Turner was there and his small Land-Rover.

———

CHAPTER 21

With Geraldine beside him Turner had driven to the other side. It meant going about 100 metres along in the other direction. They hadn't talked much, just a polite interchange about the distance, dust and the welcome river. Now Turner's tent was up too and an improvised kitchen built from saplings with a tarpaulin cover.

A dip was irresistible, and there was washing to do. Before going off by herself Geraldine saw Turner move away with the others. He wore brief navy trunks, and she liked his virile thighs and the calm way he walked and the broad shoulders and chest.

She could hear their shouts and laughter from her solitary pool fed by its own little rapid. She washed herself and her clothes and shampooed her hair. Then she tossed in the rushing water, clinging to a rock, laughing aloud with the joy of it and Turner's body and his masculinity and his touch which she would not find abhorrent.

Lunch was stale bread toasted, with peanut butter and sliced white onion. It was the last of the bread. Turner countered the raw vulgarity of the others, and Jim seemed glad to have him there. There were tins of baby food for dessert, pulped apple; Turner's contribution.

Lines of rope were put up to dry the washing. Turner had a bag of clothes pegs, enough for everyone. When two of the tents began to slip in the sand it was Turner who made longer stakes and drove them in to give the tent pegs purchase. Already the youngsters adored him. At any sudden flare-up of temper it was Turner who brought instant calm. Geraldine saw Jim as a sorry specimen beside Turner. Even the moaning of Joey or someone, an accompaniment they'd had all along because he'd forgotten his camera – even that was ended by Turner who handed over his own.

Dinner was out of cans, macaroni cheese with French beans, and sliced salami, an apple each, and coffee. Turner was part of them now.

'I'll make a damper tomorrow,' he said.

'There's no flour,' someone said.

'I've got flour.'

'Bloody fabulous!'

Geraldine thought of Julie's damper and smiled, wondering whether Turner's would have better luck. She caught Turner watching her and thought the smile they exchanged was something special that the others had no share in. The uneasy feeling Jim gave her was modified by Turner's presence.

Dusk was swift and lovely. The full fat moon came up to join the stars, the campfire threw dancing red flares on the trees and deepened mysterious shadows. Someone was turning the washed things top to bottom. It would all be dry in the morning's sun.

They sat round the fire with their instant coffee as darkness fell, then sat on. Even Geraldine. The night was too lovely to waste under cramped blue canvas and Turner was both comfort and stimulation. The kids told crazy yarns, vying with each other for Turner's approving smile. She liked the slow way he puffed his pipe. Jim was silent but seemed content, staring into the fire. She had a feeling his mind was far away.

A chill came down and they all got sweaters. She, too, returned to the fire because Turner was there. It was the sense of security he gave her. All doubts and fears would drop away

in the face of such pervading calm, and even floods and scorpions would think twice.

It was after one-thirty when Geraldine said goodnight,
leaving Jim and Turner alone by the embers. Jim's goodnight
was as pleasant as Turner's. She had an odd feeling they'd
arranged the meeting here. But that was silly: total strangers.
Turner was a self-sufficient man on a solitary trek. Thinking
of him the blue canvas was less oppressive. She drifted into
the sweet half state before sleep, where Turner was with his
quiet strength, and the sound of water, and Jim, slight beside
Turner and watchful and not going. Why did she think of
Nerida? It was like a dream, remote as a dream, unreal.
Everything a dream, all of life.

There was more organising next day. Jim seemed to want
to stay on. Turner, curiously, had an extra tent and this was
erected for the storage of food. He had a portable cooler. He
built a special fireplace to cook his dampers in, choosing a
spot between small boulders which would act as corners. He
got them to dig a pit for rubbish at a good distance from the
camp site. The youngsters loved it when he told them to toe
the line. Later in the morning he made a damper. It was
funny to watch this big man mixing and kneading at the
improvised table, getting the fire right, burying the camp
oven (his, of course) in the ground below. They had the
damper hot for lunch with real butter – Turner again, who
had it in tins. And afterwards baby foods: pulped apple and
apricot and egg custard. 'Good stuff to fall back on, never
travel without it,' Turner said. It was strange that such a sta-
ble, methodical man was so full of surprises, but they were
methodical surprises. Was he some kind of ranger or inspec-
tor? There was distance in his light grey eyes.

The day got hotter. Even in the shade there was no escaping
the smothering humidity. The others plunged into the pool to
fight off the pall of enervation. Geraldine went to the smaller
pool she'd made her own, with its own little tumbling torrent.
The shrieks of their horseplay came through the trees as if from

a vast distance, yet only a bend in the river separated them from her. She turned on her back, floating, staring up at the far pattern of leaves against deep blue. Now and again she had to nudge herself off from the bank. Once or twice she felt the slippery soft touch of a river fish. She turned over and floated face down. The water so crystal clear in the rapid was here murky and weedy, concealing the shallow bottom. Little things darted about beneath her. Something touched her left foot, but instead of slithering off it became a grip and slid up to her shin. Panic paralysed her whole body and for a crazy instant she saw Nerida's face no longer young and pretty but old with vengeance. Then power returned and Geraldine lunged and flailed with arms and legs in an effort to get rid of the deadly grip. Her mouth and eyes were full of water and she'd taken some in, but training and physical strength brought her head out of the water and she curled into a ball, wrenching her leg free.

'Hey,' a voice shouted.

Geraldine reached the bank and lay there, coughing and spluttering.

'Thought you'd had it,' the voice said. Hands came on to her shoulders.

She rolled away and sat up. It was Jim with his blank black eyes. Behind him she saw Turner's navy trunks in a hurry to get there.

She stood up and picked up her towel. Inside was a gaping pit of horror and fear, but she knew that her outward appearance was calm. She smiled at Turner.

'Trouble?' he asked in his steady voice.

'It's nothing,' Geraldine said, watching Jim, trying to fathom his expression. 'It was marvellous until the interruption.'

'Sorry,' Jim said, his eyes somewhere beyond her. 'Saw you face down and expected the worst.'

Turner smiled as if Jim were joking. 'Looks nice here,' he said. 'Hope it's not private property.

Geraldine smiled and Turner waded in, then started a careful crawl. Amused, she watched him a few moments. Then she turned, feeling Jim's absence, and saw him disappearing in the direction of camp. Geraldine sat on the bank, smiling at Turner's awkward aquatics.

Jim had meant to drown her. He might have succeeded if Turner hadn't been there. Jim had sensed Turner's approach and stopped in time. Gratitude to Turner choked in her throat.

Turner looked clumsy only because the pool was small. In real water he'd be a good performer. Grace and speed were not precluded by size. He waded out and dabbed at himself with his towel, then sat down beside Geraldine.

'That cools you off,' he said. 'Bit of a current in there.'

'My foot was pulled,' Geraldine said.

His smiled teased. 'Your leg, I think.'

Geraldine gave him a sombre look. 'I know the feel of a hand.'

Turner stared at the water. 'All sorts of things in there. I felt them myself.'

'This was human.' It could only be Jim, but she couldn't say Jim.

'Weeds.'

Did he really think her such a fool? Or was it just to reassure her? Turner was observant. He'd have seen the malice in Jim's manner. She knew Jim would try again. Her mind slid off from that.

Turner was half reclining on his elbows. Geraldine could feel his eyes. She guessed he was falling in love with her. She knew his initial interest had grown to something deeper. He watched her so. I can't bear to let you out of my sight, his face said.

'Cold?' he asked.

'Just a tremor.'

They talked idly. Turner had intended to go right to the top, but now he wasn't sure, he said. Geraldine knew it was because of her. He was falling in love as they all did: Dennis, even that vulgar drunken Clyde with his boring financial clichés.

But she had first to test him out, this man. So far he'd measured up but one didn't throw oneself at the feet of an adoring stranger, as she had with Noel. She'd learned a lesson with Noel, hadn't she? How different they were: Noel gregarious, laughing, handsome, hiding his cruelty; this Turner solitary, grave, his face just a face, but compassionate. Not much style, but a few of her touches would soon fix that.

'What made you come on the trip?' Turner asked.

'I love it so. I love the bush. I did the same thing last year but the people were awful. I missed so much, so an opportunity like this had to be grabbed. I want to remember it all, make it matter.'

'Good idea jotting things down,' he said.

Even details like that he remembered about her. She'd seen the way he looked at the others: critically, at times in open disapproval, resenting their being a part of her life, even temporarily. Then when his eyes came back to her: their intensity, their obsessive quality. Possessive too. She believed he had possession as his goal, not a body-and-soul hurtful thing but a sort of sheltering love. He'd seen the innate appeal for protection behind the fiction of size.

'You tan well,' he said with open all-over admiration.

Apart from Noel, Turner was the only man whose eyes she could bear on her body. She wanted to laugh out loud in exultation. Because it was inevitable that they'd come together. A mutual passion, a shared ecstasy, the emptiness ended. All Turner needed was a little polishing; basically he was worthy and decent and right instincts. Choosing his clothes would be fun.

'I swim a lot. I've got a pool at home.'

Would he care if he knew she'd killed Noel? But if he loved her for the person she was, why should it make any difference that she'd killed Noel? And Nerida too. Caught so many times together, such evil had to be stopped and both of them beyond reason, that silly moronic girl and Noel so remote it was a stranger sharing her bedroom. Physically wasn't enough; she wanted all of Noel. Marriage was only a small part, perhaps had fouled things up, because Noel began receding at once, even during their honeymoon. She couldn't grasp hold of him. When she wanted the strength of a rock, of a great mountain, he was elusive, the water that ran off the mountain. Even when they strained together – perhaps then most of all. He ran through her fingers, dodged the bind of her loving female web. She was left with nothing and no way to fill it up, no pretence that the nothing wasn't there.

'You're not listening,' Turner said, 'miles away.'

Geraldine adjusted her mind and smiled. 'I'm sorry, I felt so peaceful just sitting here. You're a restful person.'

'That's good,' Turner said, 'but it can't go on, can it?'

She felt a stab of terror.

'I mean,' he said, 'not with that hungry crew back there clamouring for dinner. We'd better go and pull our weight or we'll get the dishes to do.'

'Of course.' The enormous relief. What had she expected? 'What are we having tonight?' she asked, as she let him help her up.

'Some rare delicacy. Boiled potatoes, I think.'

They laughed together, wonderfully together, and started the walk back.

The fire was going, and there was a settled-in look, almost homey. The big iron pot was on the tripod with steam and a pungent smell rising from it. Another pot stuck in the coals. Afternoon light with longer shadows. Everyone busy at jobs. It was only the sight of Jim that spoiled her pleasure and started a flutter of fear.

Dressing in her tent she thought of Turner, his nice smile. She pulled on her favourite jeans, a bit too tight now, and a blue shirt that blued her hazel eyes.

I've got Turner now. Turner saved my life. I'm safe with Turner.

She took a cashmere cardigan. Paulie or someone yelled, 'Gawd, mate, visitors!' The others ran to the water's edge

waving and calling cries of welcome to the big old battered
Land-Rover that pulled up on the flat caked sand. Turner in a
white cotton sweater and grey pants joined the youngsters. An
old open car was behind the Land-Rover, much older than
some of the derelict cars along the track.

Three men in jeans, check shirts, big boots, wide-brimmed
hats and big grins stood on the other side exchanging witti-
cisms with the others. They were stockmen, they said. Two
whites and one black. In the old car an elderly dignified black
couple waited patiently.

'Me Mum and Dad,' the Aborigine introduced them. They
remained grave and silent.

Geraldine moved towards Turner. Where was Jim? She
looked round suddenly. Jim was near the trees on the other
side of their camp site. She felt his black circles watching her.

'Gawd, you're a rum-looking bunch,' one of the men said
with a laugh.

He meant, Geraldine thought, they fitted no safari pattern
he'd so far encountered. Turner, too, was cut from a different
mould.

Another old car drove down on to the flat and pulled up
facing the stockmen. It was the two fiftyish men. They got
out. The pale one paler and the red one redder. They looked
like staying.

Jim's voice right in her ear yelled to the others to come
and get stuck in. Geraldine shrank from the violence in it.
Then he said quietly, 'Mind giving the stew a stir, Mrs Blaine,
and watch the potatoes?' Her mood plunged at the dead tone
of his voice.

The stew was canned lamb and vegetables. Turner's potatoes prediction was in the other pot. Turner drained them
and threw in a knob of butter. There was tomato juice to
start with. That night she went early to her tent. Jim had
spoiled everything with fear and memory. She saw the other
men's campfire across the water. The stockmen had long
been gone.

Squeaking on the stretcher she got out her notebook. She didn't have to find words, they were burning in her head.

26 JULY: Jim is trying to kill me.

She put the notebook on the ground, switched of her torch and lay down. Their voices came subdued from the fire. The night sky sped across through the little net square.

Jim would try again.

Wisps of cloud swept at tremendous speed. The sky here was always alive, even without clouds it was always active, the stars pulsating. Even the moon was tearing across as she glimpsed it between the cloud trailers. Spectacular rents in the clouds. What a simpleton Noel must have thought her. That long ago Hawkesbury River night. Another world. Another life. It must be those thieving landlords again, he'd said. Poisonous Clyde always bellowed with laughter at Noel's puns, clever or not. It egged Noel on until they rained thick and fast, trivial and obvious. Had she been so blinded with love or had they come after marriage, like shiftiness and infidelity? Weren't puns, like knock-knees, a lifelong affliction? Perhaps he'd kept them bottled up while he skated in over the thin ice of his good fortune. Then popped the cork, safe with the income from her spectacular rents. After all, it was a serious business for Noel, getting her to the altar with all her worldly goods. Nothing punningly funny about it. One thing was sure, dear Noel's laughter was a mask for scheming cruelty.

How different was Turner. Humour, gentleness and devotion behind the gravity of his face.

She groped for the notebook and switched on her torch.

But I'm safe with Turner. He stays so close. He eyes me with such imploring longing.

It should have stopped the depression. Because of Turner she wanted life and living.

———

CHAPTER 22

She could see them go to pieces as she watched. Just like the first time. A girl in a dirty shirt of hateful pink. The river level falling to stagnant smelly pools, the stench of which blew over the pink spaghetti dished up for breakfast. She wouldn't eat their germy food. Stick to apples and her private nuts and raisins and vitamin pills.

'Sleep well?'

The organisation she thought she'd seen yesterday had been a mirage. A homey look, she'd thought. Sunlight fell on filthy cartons of food, utensils left unwashed and caked with old gravy. Fell on degeneration, on Jim with his face an inch from his dixie shovelling the stuff into his face. Geraldine got out her notebook and looked at the date on her watch.

27 JULY: Camp a revolting mess. It's falling apart. They have no staying power. Jim going downhill fast. If it weren't for Turner –

She stopped. She'd forgotten Turner. She looked for him. They were watching her, all of them. Their eyes saw her writing and didn't like it. Turner was watching her too but differently, a grave smile on his grave face.

'Sleep well?' he asked again.

'Raving bloody ratbag, if you ask me,' someone said.

'Yes, thank you,' Geraldine said.

The ratbag person got up, a male, she thought, and started skipping away.

'Chores first,' Jim called. Pink slime from the tinned spaghetti all over his face.

'Get stuffed,' the person shouted back and ran off over the nearest outcrop of rock.

The night's scraps of vapour had gone leaving the sky cloudless again.

Jim said, 'Like fishing, Mrs Blaine?'

Geraldine smiled at the sky in disdain.

'Mind washing up, then? We need a bit of order around here.'

Geraldine wrote again in her notebook.

He takes it out on me when things go wrong. His own lack of discipline enrages him. Rage is always stupid.

She shut the notebook and put it away in her bag with the pen. 'Yes, all right,' she said with a tolerant smile. Anything to make him go. Everything about Jim made her uneasy. She looked for Turner but couldn't see him. Perhaps gone to his Land-Rover for fishing gear.

The others got up and stretched, disseminating odours. They began drifting away. She waited for Jim to go too. She felt detached from the camp site, a sort of hazy feeling that came with depression. Only Jim's brooding face unsettled her, and the malignancy he directed only at her. She had a sinking conviction they were stuck in this camp for ever, that she could do nothing about advance or retreat, that Jim would go on with his bewildering persecution. She knew there was a goal for her somewhere, the only thing that mattered, but this morning it was far away.

Jim got up at last.

Soon, left alone, she'd clean up the camp so that their silly mouths would drop open. It was nice to retain sanity, to know that when they cracked apart she'd be the calm and rational one. The enormous pity she felt; how kind she'd been to the others, how nice, and Jim knew it deep down. So to be called a raving ratbag – and of course it was meant for her, the different one, the one whose standards couldn't be made to slip. It was so irrational it was amusing. But, all the same, irritating.

They thought her not much use. It was lucky for them they had her level head along, the mature outlook Jim had seen as so essential for the trip. They thought her round the bend and, by their lights, she was. In Sydney it had been the same. Dennis had laughed at the watch she kept on Noel. It was true she brooded on anything that took Noel's attention: his job, his mail, his friends; his taste in food or books or paintings that differed from her own. But that was love, wasn't it? Dennis knew it, so had gone out of his way to make her jealous, when all the time she'd known Noel was as all-male as a man could be. Poor Dennis wanting her for himself, finding solace in Noel-proximity. Clyde was the same, dragging Noel off to pornographic movies because Geraldine didn't hide her repugnance for him.

She saw the fiftyish men go off with guns. How peaceful now with everyone gone. Only flies and blowflies, and up in the free sky the free birds.

Apple peelings, prune stones, damper crumbs, the pale pink slimy worms of uneaten spaghetti and other refuse all into the bucket, then the bucket to Turner's rubbish pit. Then a spade spreading a layer of sand to baffle the blowflies. There was plenty of hot water and liquid detergent. The blurriness in her head got her through. Mrs Mac called it buckling down. It was the faraway feeling that followed hurt and confusion, where mechanical chores could be tackled with dispatch. Dear Mrs Mac, holding the fort. When it was done Geraldine cleaned the bowl with Vim. It would nice never to see them again. Except Turner. She was hurt that Turner had gone. She replaced the food in Turner's food tent. He must have a first name. There were distant rifle shots. The drinking water was dwindling in the cooler. She found the broom and swept the sand flat, picking up the cigarette butts. The sand glittered with a million pinpoints of mica. She took six tea-towels down to the river to wash, then hung them on the line with Turner's pegs. The neat and orderly look of everything pleased her.

She sat down in the shade. It was strange how the quiet was filled with a sound that was silence; every noisy bird a part of the still and waiting bush. Only human sound jarred and shattered. The others thought her a spoilsport. Would they appreciate the housekeeping she'd done? Would they even notice? Noel could never call her a spoilsport. Every time she'd be there in the thick of idiotic pursuits with her face of enjoyment that no one could fault. Why were her interests never on the agenda? Too quiet and personal and solitary: reading, music, gardening, her household pottering. Noel took it for granted they didn't count in group fun. Of course he was right. And perhaps deep inside she had the makings of a spoilsport in Noel's sense, which was why she took such extraordinary teeth-gritting care. Well, she'd found a new interest, or rather had it gratuitously bestowed by Noel, because it was Noel's doing to make them die, not her plan, she hadn't thought of their dying, it had happened so, it had to happen. Noel had thrust her into a situation and a set of feelings and emotions and even intellectual attitudes foreign to the person she was. The way out had been forced on her, not sought by her. But she'd survived, hadn't she? and would go on surviving.

The clean camp rested her mind, it pleased her sense of order. Gone the grubby chaos of breakfast-time.

It was the memory of Jim's breakfast face that gave her the idea. She went to the food tent. A carton of canned spaghetti was still half full. Carrying six at a time, she took them down the slope at the back of the site that led to a dry gully, probably an arm of the river that in full flood would be one with it. She buried the cans under loose sand and dry leaves. It took several trips. Down on her haunches she smoothed the leaves and sand to a natural look.

'Burying the body?'

Geraldine jumped. She looked up at Turner but he was smiling. It was a joke. 'Worse than that,' she said, 'the spaghetti.'

'What, all of it?'

'Every last tin.' She stood up and brushed her hands together, smiling.

'That's an extreme measure.' She liked the twinkle in his eyes. He carried a fishing-rod but seemed fishless.

'Extreme suffering demands extreme measures.'

'You don't like spaghetti?'

'*Real* spaghetti.'

'It's not so bad. It makes a change. It's a useful extra.'

She hoped he wasn't going to trot out a lot of clichés. He'd come up from the gully, he'd had a longish glimpse. How silent he'd been. 'Where did you spring from?'

'Stumbled on a back way round.'

'I'm glad you're back. No fish?'

'The youngsters got some yabbies.'

They walked up the slope to the camp site.

'My,' Turner said, 'you've made a transformation here.'

It pleased Geraldine inordinately, although she'd known Turner would appreciate things, notice things.

'The water's getting low,' she said.

'Enough till tomorrow. Jim's pushing on tomorrow. Nice bloke, Jim.'

'Are you coming with us?'

'Jim said it's okay – all right with you?'

'I'm surprised you ask,' she said with her loveliest, warmest smile.

'Had a swim?' he asked.

'I'm going now. Will you come too?'

'You go on. I'll join you. Just get rid of this gear and a couple of things.'

It was appallingly hot and humid, but Geraldine flew through clean cool exhilarating air. Everything was good; bad things didn't exist. She heard the fiftyish brutes shooting their brutal shots and shut her mind to them. In the black swimsuit she'd worn for Nerida, with her towel, she felt herself a nymph flitting through the trees to their private pool. Turner was coming with them. With Turner close she was safe. If Turner thought Jim was a nice bloke, that was all right with her. Jim didn't matter. Now Turner was in her life nothing else mattered. Perhaps she'd misjudged Jim. She'd thought him reserved, but instead he was surly. It was easy to misjudge people. She felt magnanimous. Jim was a mystery, that was all, he kept his own counsel. It was that she'd liked about him.

It seemed hours she had to wait. After washing herself in the little rapid she swam round and round the pool, then turned on her back and floated, watching for his thighs through the trees. It was delicious to float with shut eyes. Fun to nudge the bank and push off again, to feel through shut eyelids the flickers of sunlight through trees.

'You're a widow, Mrs Blaine.'

It was a shock. His voice so close. It wasn't a question. Gossipy Jim. It maddened her that they'd been talking about her. She'd been wrong about Jim's reserve. She opened her eyes and smiled. He was on the bank right above her. With a lithe movement she was out and dripping beside him. He handed her the towel.

'Yes.' She rubbed her hair vigorously, tossed it back and smiled at him. Then she towelled her body. Gossipy Jim. 'Jim told you?'

'Somebody mentioned it.' He sat down and began to fill his pipe. He was still dressed. Hadn't he said a swim? Of course it was Jim who told him; this was just Turner being ungossipy.

She sat down near him. 'Yes, I've been lonely.'

After a pause he said, 'I know the feeling. After my wife called it a day – ' he stopped.

Geraldine thought his wife mad to leave Turner. 'My husband died very suddenly, a car crash.'

'Good driver?'

'Yes – well – no, not really, erratic. He could handle a car, but he was overconfident, careless, and then drinking.'

'The usual combination.'

They sat in silence for a while. How restful he was, so strong, so undemanding. And so sad. And so understanding.

'He got in with the wrong sort of crowd,' she said suddenly.

Turner puffed and nodded.

Geraldine told Turner of the good position her husband had when they married. 'With an excellent firm, and contented until he ran into – ran into these others.' She gave Turner her views on advertising people, on selfish whims and impulses, on crowded little corner restaurants where the liquor licence carried more weight than the food. Turner was a sympathetic listener. A drink was all right in its place, he said. What Turner said was trite enough, but it was Turner saying it that gave it significance. For the first time Geraldine knew the meaning of empathy.

She went on talking. Found herself telling Turner things she'd kept bottled up so long, like the pitfalls of marriage, the ease of infidelity – things Turner knew about, didn't he? It was an impulse she didn't want to control. She could feel the bond between them: his wife, her husband, and something else, something immediate sprung to life. And besides, Turner was so *other*, so nothing to do with her former life. From another world, a different existence, met by chance in such unlikely circumstances: Land-Rovers on the way up to Cape York Peninsula. So it was like talking on to a tape, for fun, for erasure. Remote, as the feeling she got in her head thinking about Noel.

'So this trip was a godsend,' Turner said.

'It helped the loneliness.'

'I know your area well, all the eastern suburbs. Wasn't there a double murder recently in Woollahra?'

Geraldine caught her breath. Slowly she said, 'I don't know.'

Then added in a rush, 'In June there were two sordid deaths' – she paused and corrected herself – 'or however long ago it was.'

'June is correct,' Turner said. 'What happened, exactly?'

Geraldine's smile was disparaging. 'It all sounded very novelettish, an ageing married man and a young girl. Perhaps he killed her and then committed suicide.'

'Ever met them, know them at all?'

Geraldine felt her face go funny, but knew her voice was steady. 'Heavens, no, not my kind of people. It all sounds so loose and untidy and dirty.'

Turner nodded in sympathy. 'Remember their names?'

'No.' Noel and Nerida, both dead, all their lovely living lost for ever.

'And no one was charged?'

Geraldine shivered.

'Cold?' Turner asked, at once solicitous.

'A bit shivery; this damp towel.'

Turner took her arm as she stood up. 'Thoughtless of me, you'd better get something on.'

Walking back Geraldine said, 'You know what I'd like?'

'What?' he smiled down at her.

'All the others to vanish and you and I go on.'

Turner laughed and said, 'It may come to that.'

In the afternoon he made two dampers and hard-boiled some eggs. The others were in high spirits; they'd seen a wallaby, chased a goanna and cooked and eaten the yabbies they'd caught. Taking the tea-towels from the line Geraldine saw the fiftyish men plucking the bush turkey they'd murdered.

'We're pushing on tomorrow.'

She swung around. Jim had crept up behind her. 'Yes, I know.' Did he notice her breathless voice? Frightening things are worse in daylight. In the dark you expect them.

'Good,' he said. 'We'll start early.'

Everything seemed unreal. Geraldine went to the tent to pack. Even the weather – a change was coming over the day. The others had gone for a last exploration of the river. Later on when she came out Turner and Jim were talking, lolling about on the sand. Or rather Jim was talking, Turner's sympathetic ear now turned to Jim. Her depression grew. Since Turner's questions on the river bank the image of death had stuck in her head. Turner of all people, the kindest of men, reviving the horror. Jim was nodding his head at Turner. He liked having Turner with them; he too depended on Turner.

The others came back noisier than ever. They'd met a man who owned a station some kilometres up river. There were baby crocs up there. December to June the road was impassable. He'd lost a herd of horses and cattle in the last flood. His raft broke up and they were all caught in the treetops. This was the second biggest river up here, after the Jardine up at the top. It emptied into Archer Bay in the Gulf of Carpentaria.

What they said deepened Geraldine's desolation. It sounded unreal; they looked unreal. Motor-bikes roared through on the hard sand opposite, but they too were figures in a dream.

Scrambled eggs and fried onions.

Turner caught up with her as she reached her tent.

'I'd like to read your record of the trip some time; be interesting to check with mine.'

She knew every stone, twig, flower, mosquito. 'I think you'd be bored; it's more or less nonsense, just for my own amusement. Goodnight.'

'Goodnight,' he said.

Vulnerable in the little blue tent. Jim made her afraid. He'd tried to kill her and would try again. She was glad of Turner. She got out the notebook and sat on the side of the stretcher. But instead of opening it she got ready for bed. She felt shivery. And wind from the onions.

The day must come when Jim would be over and done with.

———

CHAPTER 23

Morning came cold and without sun. Everyone goosey. Geraldine demolished her own tent. Brown owls, red leaves, slummocky packing. Doom-cry of crows in the silent bush.

'Mad, yer bugger!'

'Who says so?'

'Jeez, the bites are bad!'

'Where's the bloody spaghetti?'

Breakfast was hot macaroni out of cans. The muddle of departure, then at last they were off. Geraldine couldn't stop shivering. The sun was pale, hiding behind a cold greyish veil that lay over everything. A cyclone coming? They gave them names like Hetty and Tillie.

Turner had suggested she travel with him, but Jim said, 'Let's leave things as they are.' The black circles of eyes unreadable.

The jolts again. In places the dust become mud after showers. Detours where the track was obliterated, the Rovers mowing through the bush. Then a sort of giant prairie with roof-high bronze-brown grass like spears that swept the vehicles clean of mud and dust. The road fork hard to see, the signpost illegible. Jim kept ahead. She said nothing. It was last year's way that led to the coast. The road to the top branched left and looked a sidetrack. He'd wanted her experience and had spurned it. Well, her goal was independent of his stupidity.

Erosion so that the roots of trees wove a thin intricate mat. Parts that were deep holes, and Jim driving at a steep angle so that she fell sideways on to him. Hating it. Jim too. Their lips tight in distaste. And the near-perpendicular walls of dry creek beds or sluggish green unmoving rivers. The flying things, the anthills changing colour with the earth. And the sun back in full glare. Big yellow flowers in the spare grass, big yellow sun blazing.

A stagnant muddy river with high banks. Geraldine remembered the horror of slow things flying in the tense night of last year's camp. The map said the Wenlock River. They'd been four hours doing about 50 kilometres.

Yet Jim seemed in a hurry. To reach what? Impatient with the forced halts, with each pioneering delay. Did Jim have some purpose?

Sometimes her own goal wavered, sometimes ahead, sometimes already past. She thought she'd seen it as they died. At the moment of death seen it all solved. The long, long waiting, the moment by agonising moment: shouldn't that preponderance of life resolve itself into some kind of achievement? She thought of Turner, calm and resigned to whatever came.

Flowers scarce but flies in plenty. The heat thick in the still bush, thick in the Land-Rover, stickying everything. Slippery clay, bumps, holes, stone, a teasing maniac track through the antique bush. The big yellow single flowers again. Losing the way, poor Edmund Kennedy's road, searching for faint wheel marks in the dirty sand.

Two thirty-five and no lunch. They were chopping saplings to cross a creek.

'How about grub?' Chrissie or someone said.

'Soon as we're over this.' Jim's torso ran with sweat.

28 JULY: On my groundsheet in the shade. My hair in the glass looks shiny and neat. The others out in the blistering sun. Noel would turn back here. Back to that bitch.

Turner gave them each a hard-boiled egg.

'No salt?' someone grumbled.

'It's in there if you want it, in the big shaker.' The biscuit girl jerked her thumb at her vehicle. She had an endless supply. Each time she jumped from the Land-Rover a great shower of biscuit crumbs came with her.

'I'll get it,' Geraldine said, winning the usual hostile stares. The Land-Rover reeked of armpits. She found the salt at the top of a carton and gave it to the grumbling person.

She smiled at Turner. 'You all right?' he said.

'I'm fine, an old hand.' She felt remote from Turner and that was sad and wrong, but she couldn't lift out of the fog that shut them all off, Turner too.

On the other side of the creek they had the rest of the hard-boiled eggs, dry damper and cans of baby apple. And the instant coffee they'd brought in Thermos flasks. Then onwards again.

'You okay?' Jim said.

'Fine. You?'

'I'm okay.'

Soon the earth rising, the landscape changing, the anthills gone. Up to Iron Range, then between the black peaks and down through the rain forests. She knew every giant tree, every twist of their trunks, each insinuating frond, all the mysterious deeps of the steamy river.

Jim stopped at some crossroads and got out. He walked back. Soon she heard an engine start and saw Turner's Land-Rover moving away on the other road. Was Turner dropping out?

Jim came back. When they were on the move he said, 'Ralph's gone to the post office. He'll follow us later.'

Ralph? Geraldine giggled and felt Jim's look. Turner was Turner; no other name fitted him. Then she wanted to cry because Turner was on such intimate terms with Jim. Turner trusted Jim. Should she warn Turner? The post office? Did he expect letters? Was he writing to somebody dear to him?

They got to the little coast town of Portland Roads. Jim got out and spoke to a man on the wharf. The others ran about everywhere, over the pebbles to the sea, on to the long, rickety, resounding jetty, along to the mangroves that hedged off a snowy beach. The man with Jim pointing back over the peaks, then north up the coast, shaking his head and looking important and solemn. Jim was learning he'd taken the wrong fork all those creek crossings ago. He left the man then and she lost sight of him among fibro and weatherboards.

It was nice to stroll about and feel her strong muscles. She was in better condition than any of them, except perhaps Turner. It was physical health that produced clarity of thought, kept alive the sense of purpose.

There were holiday people drinking beer. A woman with a small girl and two plastic bowls was washing clothes at the tap by the jetty. She saw the big yellow truck of a mining company. The sun was heading down into the range. She read the memorial to poor Kennedy. Jim came and she heard him shout to the others. He got them to fill the water drums at the tap.

'We'll look for a place to camp,' he said, 'and step on it.'

They started back up the road. She felt no interest in his plans. In Sydney she'd thought him kind, even intelligent, outstanding among Noel's poisonous crew. Now she knew that Jim, too, fell to pieces in rough-going.

It was ironically right to camp in the same clearing as last year. The same rusted petrol drums, the same giant ants.

The same unloading and pitching of tents, their blue so like the orange. Turner came in the middle of it, bringing stores from Iron Range. Jim had left a stick in a can as a marker for Turner, although it would be hard to miss such a mess as was there already.

It was almost dark. The others fell on the fresh bread likes wolves on a lamb. Turner in the light of lanterns was already busy with his neat housekeeping. Tomorrow he'd rig up a kitchen bench. While he got dinner the others with their torches on had lots of fun peeling the young paperbarks, competing for the longest strip. The flickering lights intensified the dreamlike quality all things had.

Dinner was oyster soup to start, then a stew of cans with potatoes, then nuts and muscatels from a weevily packet. Turner had got powdered milk, eggs, marmalade and raisins. Tomorrow he'd make a brownie, which he said was a damper with raisins in it. Turner had a satisfied look as if something pleased him, perhaps news he'd picked up at the post office. An air of languor hung about. The others begged to stay at least two nights, and Jim said maybe three with so much to do, like petrol and stuff. He discussed the route with Turner, saying he thought they should push on up the coast. Turner nodded. They didn't consult Geraldine.

Only she knew that the road to come was the worst going of all. It would demoralise all of them. Turner too? Perhaps. Jim's face grew thinner and longer every day. The others had youth to make light of obstructions: root and rocks, ants and shortages and monotonous diet, holdups, the dust and mud and heat and stinging bites. But youth was inexperience, and they'd soon find it was the little things that grew insuperable. It might be fun to watch them come unstuck. It wasn't enough to be young, expectant, illusioned. They were without thought and reason, too young for Geraldine as she was too old for them. A century too old. Different worlds. They lived now, Geraldine in the past with only the future. Better old, with the rightness of a single goal ahead.

In the privacy between her tent and Land-Rover she managed a total wash. An old hand. Only the fat old moon watching. She could hear them talking, all unwashed with their low voices round the fires. Dark and distance made it a friendly sound. Deodorised, scented, in jeans, shirt and brushed hair, she sat on the stretcher and got out the notebook, at once forgetting what had seemed important. It didn't matter. Had Turner said he'd like to read her record? His would be a dull catalogue of weather and distance, with none of the detail her organized mind captured.

The circle round the fire seemed designed to exclude her. Geraldine sat in the half dark on her groundsheet. Jim's face looked shifty in the orange glow, and his blue eyes fell away from her after a swift look. Turner was talking, puffing on his pipe and keeping the others amused with one of the yarns they seemed to find so absorbing. Geraldine was silent, feeling sad. Turner made her sad. She wanted to talk and laugh with him, feel close like yesterday. It was sad that he was suddenly dreary, fiddling with his eggs and raisins and yesterday already too long ago.

Five minutes or two hours later she got up and went to bed, forgetting to say goodnight.

Even up here with everything ended the fantasies came into her tent. It was over, past, dead, yet still they came to torment her, drifting in through the little net square like innocent night vapours. Jealousy, the feeling of being unwanted, being tricked. Right from the first, slippery Noel. Dennis, Clyde, Claire, Elaine, and all the long list of imagined ones so much worse than the known. Then at last Nerida and Noel's final trickery. Geraldine knew at the very first glimpse, the very same evening of the day she got back that other time, right then at that moment she knew it was to be Nerida. Nerida was Noel's ending of it between them. Well, now it was ended for Noel and for Nerida too. As Paulie or Vinnie would say: they'd had it. It was silly Nerida who showed Geraldine the waste of her former jealousies. So why now let them torment her, and why let Nerida? Geraldine had the last laugh, and logic, and security.

I'm safe. Only this trip to see through. But I'm safe.

It would be nice now when the trip was done. She'd proved her superiority over past and present. The point she must reach might be a slow awakening, an understanding taking time. Not the moment of clarity she'd sought with Noel. Being alone was altogether different. But in any form it would mean her mastery of the future, too.

Tomorrow would be washing day for all of them. And she no longer had to hear how lucky she was to have Noel. That was something to smile about.

CHAPTER 24

Two snakes and a goanna. The damp sea wind. Everyone's laundry strung up with Turner's pegs. Hair washed in the public shower shed on the wharf. Coastal steamers and a bird as big as an albatross, but Turner said it wasn't. Oysters growing beneath the jetty. A green parrot with red cheeks, stationary in a bare tree. The petrol done. Two big lizards and another snake. Turner's brownie baked. Jim intent on something inside himself. Lavatory paper added to the shopping list. The others late for lunch from their swim, three with queasy tummies. In the middle of baked beans and sauerkraut another safari saying hello, all-male all round Australia. After lunch the others off again, mad for bird watching.

In her tent Geraldine put on the black swimsuit. It was the only one she'd brought and she called it Nerida's. Turner had suggested a swim. Jim was coming too, but with Turner there she was safe. She picked up her switch to beat at the flies and went outside.

Jim and Turner were washing up and talking. She moved towards them.

Jim said, 'Poor bloke, he enjoyed living, that was all he asked, just life with its ups and downs.' The dead black circles hid Jim's eyes. 'Being married to a zombie was no help.'

'Did he ever think of leaving her?' Turner said.

'Scared to, I reckon.'

Geraldine exchanged a smile with Turner. His eyes were on her body beneath the shorts and shirt and she recognised the longing in them.

'And your girl was the opposite?' Turner said.

'Full of life, concerned about everything.' Jim stared down at the washing-up bowl. 'I didn't mind the affair, it wasn't important. We understood each other. It was just a flash in the pan; we both knew that. There'd been others; it didn't interfere with the thing we had together.'

Geraldine stopped listening. What a bore. She slashed at the flies. Couldn't they leave this drivel till later and come for a swim if they were coming? Jim took the bowl and tipped the water out into the trees. Turner stacked the clean things away and Jim came back.

Turner said, 'His wife didn't see it that way.'

Jim kicked a stone aside. His eyes met Geraldine's, she thought. He smiled. She hadn't seen him smile in a long time. Poor Jim, perhaps after all he had some finer feelings. 'What do you think, Mrs Blaine?'

'I don't know what you're talking about.' She took a swipe at a dragonfly and missed.

They were both watching her. Then Turner said to Jim, 'You ready?'

'Just get into my swimming trunks,' Jim said. He went off to his tent.

Geraldine mooched about, bored, hot, the humidity starting a trickling inside the swimsuit. She whipped the leaves of a sapling. Turner came up beside her and smiled.

'Be nice to cool off,' he said.

Geraldine folded her switch double then let the tip spring back.

'It would be a shock,' Turner said, 'two sudden deaths so close.'

Geraldine shrugged. 'Would it?' What had she to do with their silly talk.

'You're not interested?' Turner smiled.

Geraldine said in a flat voice, 'I suppose it's a shock to you when a shock doesn't shock.'

Turner said nothing, just watched her.

'That's not a pun, is it?' The thought made her smile.

'No,' Turner said. Then he said, 'You mean it's no shock because death's so commonplace?'

'I suppose so.' Who cared? Why did he go on and on? With his eyes eating her up because he was so crazy for her?

Turner said, 'Death's always a shock to me, in ones or millions.'

His earnestness was a bore. She thought for a moment he looked a detective again, but knew it was only the context. 'I'll get my bag,' she said, and left him abruptly. On the way she swung at a yellow daisy and scored a bull's eye. An epigram what she'd said, perhaps? An aphorism? One of those things.

Some instinct kept her in her tent until she heard the engine start. Turner was in the back and her place beside Jim waiting for her. She got in and put towel and handbag on her knees.

On the way Jim said, 'My girl would've loved this trip.' He seemed to be talking to himself, or to the red road.

Turner's voice came. 'She'd feel justified, you know, the wife. Feel she was right, exacting justice. We had a schizo bloke did much the same a couple of years ago.'

'I'll be glad when she gets what's coming,' Jim said in a savage voice.

Geraldine felt a surge of compassion for Jim. Not because of his girl but because he let it eat him up. He couldn't unbend. You'd think up here, a continent away – it was puzzling that anyone could so give in to self-pity. She edged towards him. 'I'm terribly sorry about your girl,' she said in a soft voice.

Jim flinched as though he'd been stung. Geraldine shifted back. He was bent on being a boor, so that was that.

Turner said, 'These other youngsters knew her?'

'Yes,' Jim said, 'loved her, too, everyone loved Nerida. She was that kind of girl. Even her parents came round after she'd – '

Geraldine stopped listening. It wasn't Jim talking, her mind was making it up, like other odd thoughts she'd had of late. There was the sea, they were pulling up, and people about.

But Jim went on driving slowly along the sea front.

She saw the truth far off, so remote it had no meaning: Jim's dead girl was Nerida; he'd been in love with Nerida. Jim was Nerida's, Nerida Jim's. It didn't matter. Nothing mattered. She was cocooned in cotton wool, safe from these silly men, safe from everything.

Jim found a parking place and stopped. 'Water looks good,' he said. They got out. They started down to the beach.

She'd thought it all out so well, as she always thought things out to the last detail before taking action.

The sea was a washed-out turquoise. Jim ran in first, diving seawards. When he came up he struck out but took only a few strokes, then turned and bobbled as people do. Not much of a swimmer. She was ready now, her toes digging into the sand. Turner was fussily folding his shorts and shirt and making sure his pipe was safe. Geraldine felt strong, knew that despite the weight she'd put on her strength was undiminished. She ran in and struck out, fast as a fish, as lightning, a dolphin, an avenging angel. Jim had moved further out. She saw his head in front of her, in profile. Geraldine rolled over, saw Turner trundling awkwardly into the sea.

She dived under. She saw Jim's legs but in that instant they moved; not in alarm, just a few kicks to keep himself afloat. The sea was shallow. One could stand here and the sea would be no more than breast-high. Geraldine stayed under. Jim's legs idled again, his feet turned shoreward; probably he was watching Turner's careful wadings. Geraldine surfaced, floated, turned and dived again. Swift and straight as an arrow she went for Jim's legs, gripped one and came up beside him, laughing. Jim's face was half fear, half anger. Turner was still some distance away, in no hurry. Geraldine went under again but this time she took Jim with her in a relentless grip. She had his thighs. He struggled and beat at her in a futile watery way, his mouth open. Geraldine smiled with tight-shut lips and watched his struggles and willed him with her eyes to give up the ghost. She felt no malice towards Jim. All she saw was Nerida with Noel, two bodies too close, overlapping. Jim was something to do with it, that was all. Her strong fingers pressed harder.

Then the unexpected happened. Strange big hands got hold of Jim and took him up. Geraldine let go and surfaced. Turner was holding Jim behind the shoulders, keeping his head above water, and Turner's eyes were watching her.

Geraldine gasped and took in gusts of air. She felt the look of relief on her face. 'Oh, thank heaven,' she said in a breathless voice, 'I thought he'd gone.'

'Guessed you'd need help,' Turner said. Then he took Jim as a lifesaver does and swam towards shore. Geraldine didn't follow, didn't watch. Instead she enjoyed the water, not the worst she'd swam in. Even the burning sun was benign in water. She floated and turned lazily, her head empty, her body enjoying every sensation the water gave her. At last when she'd had enough she turned shorewards.

They weren't on the beach. Geraldine towelled herself. They'd mussed up her things. She picked up shorts and shirt and put on her sunglasses. Then she went up to the Land-Rover. It was empty. A glance all round the waterfront showed they were out of sight.

Delayed panic swamped her. She saw the trap they'd set. She could take the Land-Rover. Now, take it now. With a four-wheel drive she could cope with any hazard. The others were out in the bush goggling at birds, Turner and Jim gone off somewhere. It was astonishing they'd left such a chance to her. She was on the driver's side. She got in, dumped her things on the seat beside her. She looked at the gears and dashboard. Simple as pie.

Turner's head popped up on the other side. 'Jim won't be long,' he said in an easy voice, 'just gone for a few provisions.'

Geraldine stared at him. How funny she hadn't thought to look. She smiled. There'd be another opportunity, back at the camp, perhaps, before the others got back. But would they ever leave her alone now? She slid across to the passenger's seat.

'Lucky we were there,' Turner said with a straight look.

'Yes, wasn't it,' Geraldine said, 'I could have managed alone but I'm glad you came.'

'Give you a shock?'

'I'm always ready for emergencies in water.'

'Good way to be. Just the same you look pretty done in – not just today, it's all the time.'

'Don't we all? Who's in the pink in these conditions?'

Jim came back, opaque-eyed, silent as ever. He dumped a piled-up carton in the back. Turner got in, then Jim beside her, slamming the door. They returned to camp in silence, broken only when Jim said about halfway, 'Ralph's a champion swimmer.'

Turner's Land-Rover was parked nearest the road. If not this afternoon, then perhaps in the night. The chance would come; sometime they'd leave her alone. She saw herself driving off, away from the dreadful disarray they were creating. In times of stress of danger she was able to stand at a distance and see herself act rightly. As she had with Nerida. And then Noel.

She took off Nerida's swimsuit then washed and dressed and went outside. Turner was peeling potatoes and onions, and Jim was stacking the fire. Geraldine sat at the edge of the clearing. They took no notice of her. She felt a long way off yet conscious of every detail, every movement, every word. Turner washed the vegetables. Jim filled the billies and kettle with water. They weighed the desirability of lamb against beef stew, both in cans, as if it were of great moment, as if it weren't donkey or kangaroo. Turner got out his little book and wrote something in it, then he got out his pipe, filled it, and started his tiresome puffing. Jim was motionless on his haunches chewing a blade of grass. He had bruises on both thighs.

Geraldine felt sorry for them. For Turner too: not much education, a really awful accent, eyes too pale and wasn't he mite untrustworthy, like Noel?

I never want to see a tent again.

It was strange, the little things that hinged upon each other and led to chaos. If Noel hadn't handled the advertising he wouldn't have gone to the agency, there'd have been no Dennis or Clyde, no hare-brained eatery, no meeting with Don and no Peninsula trip. Noel wouldn't have turned back. There'd have been no Nerida. It would all have been as it was. No Jim, no second time, no Turner. Dodgy strangers had her trapped in a wilderness all because of Noel's added responsibility and switch in advertising agencies.

The others back, noisy and healthy, tummies gone. Bursting with wonders. A tree python, coiled and comfy and unconcerned. Immense coloured birds. A dear old dentist retired in a shack shared with snakes and flying foxes. Geraldine felt such pity for them, smiling at their jokes and silly young experiences, among them but watching from far off. Her jolly campfire voice offering to wash up got grateful surprised looks. Exhausted, they turned in early. They were so young, so unsubtle. And Jim and Turner, weren't they just as obvious? Trying to match her superiority without a shred of evidence? How silly of Jim to prowl over there in the shadows. And of Turner to puff his smelly old pipe and think himself invisible.

After finishing the chores, skimping nothing, Geraldine put more wood on the fire for the absurd plotters and went serenely to her tent.

Turner's voice closed in behind. 'You all right?'

She turned her smile. 'Of course.'

'Just that you look exhausted, as if it's all catching up.'

'I'm seasoned.'

'We're off in the morning, Jim wants to get ahead.'

'Good night.' She went into her tent.

Silly Jim. What was ahead that wasn't here? Or anywhere? Only rougher going. She knew exactly. Would he want to go on when he found her gone in the morning? She wouldn't undress, just sit on the stretcher, listening. They wouldn't stay up all night, at some time they'd be offguard. How silly they were, how absurd everyone. The world. Couldn't they see it was all nothing? Just an emptiness? Nations hurrying the ending. Turner too just another trekker, nothing. He would go back as she would, to nothing.

Leaves of paperbarks whispering, and a sharper, edgy sound from the gums. She knew the difference between leaves and human malice. Was it the sea faint and far away, that regular thudding? All the sounds had a rhythm. She lay down for a moment, just a moment. The bush was so soothing, so sleepy, so kind and wise. So free from silliness.

That last New Year's Eve party, in the dark of Nerida's year: the fatuities of New Year wishes for happiness and success in a world gone mad, because even Geraldine with tight-shut eyes and ears refusing to be involved in anything but Noel – even Geraldine knew the world was mad. People the last thing counting in a world gone mad. Hating to know, Geraldine knew, and longed for the pure, personal environment that should contain just herself and Noel. Happy New Year! All drunkenly rolling, Noel as drunk as Clyde. And Nerida's sly smile.

Then New Year's Day. The desolation of a public holiday in the empty city because she wouldn't join in Noel's hangover party. Had to escape. Hating, regretting in the empty streets among the last night's sordid debris, among the tatty expensive boutiques shut behind iron grilles in the shopping arcades. But finally glad. Noel's parties might turn into anything: drink, sex, boredom (always that), shouts, inanity, splittings-up into pairs: unlikely transitory couplings. Except Noel and Nerida, not unlikely at all, not transitory.

In a torturous sleep Geraldine forgot about getting up, and in the morning forgot to remember.

———

CHAPTER 25

The track that was just a rutted path, overgrown in places, in others so badly eroded the ruts were holes, often deep and long, and meshed across with fibrous roots of the tough growth. It had to be tough to cling to the edge of the barren peninsula in the rotting Pacific wind. They moved at a snail's pace, stopping often to hack leafy branches that gave the wheels purchase. Sometimes a small destructive detour. Geraldine was hot and bored; she'd done it all before, hadn't she? It seemed to go on for ever, the track, into old age, to the end of the world, into eternity. But a peninsula has an end. It has a point. That's the whole point. Geraldine smiled at the old pun so close to the extremity.

One could end it oneself. Turn back as Noel had. Give up the sweaty dusty days. But that would negate purpose. The others would crack before Geraldine cracked; already they were crumbling. Staying power is short in a long monotony.

She'd come this way before, lost after losing Noel. This was her second time, alone with Turner and Jim. The others not counting. Thank God for Jim, she'd thought at the start, having no warning.

This endless road must end somewhere. The peaks were passing, isolated ones in front diminishing to a flat distance. Nothing to break the monotony but the sea's monotony. She missed Noel physically. Meaning nothing, it was the only something she'd had. He smiled and teased, his hands caressed, he pressed his panting body into hers. Didn't he know it was two ghosts, that Noel and Geraldine never, never touched? Yet even that nothing she ached for, that worse desolation than this of the journey.

The others were cracking, the crunch was near. There'd been scenes this morning, shouts and sulking. They saw no fun in moving on so soon. Fun was something they'd very soon run out of. The road was getting them down, the constant halts.

All these hours for a few kilometres. Was this Jim's goal, the low mangrovey coastline? There was a river. They went to look at it. But not Geraldine who seemed to have seen it before. She sat in the Land-Rover with the door open, smelling the rotting stink of the stagnant river and vegetation. When they came back some decision had been made; the business of setting up camp began. Jim had called a halt. Was he planning another attempt on her life? A quiver of anger at Turner started, at the ambiguity of his presence. Yet she was ready for any move Jim might make. Was he as ready? Jim might have an accident; in terrain of this sort there were a hundred natural possibilities. And there were contrivances.

Jim knows and is out to get me.

Geraldine opened her bag for the notebook but when she couldn't find it the impulse died.

This second time had been necessary. Soon it would all be over, soon a new life.

I never want to see a tent again.

This was the last stage of a nightmare.

'Get moving – think you're bloody royalty?'

Was it Paulie's sweaty young face looking at her with such contempt? Geraldine smiled.

'There's plenty to do before it gets dark.' He stamped off with long dull hair limp about his neck.

Geraldine joined in the work, amused at their shortcomings and their resentment that she had none. Just like the first time. Funny and sad. How coarse their angry voices while the tents went up and wood was got and Turner superintended the disposition of things and Jim unshaven went to pieces, tight with a rage.

'Any more of this bloody road I've had it,' somebody said.

'How we gonna get over that stinking river? It's a kilometre wide.'

Turner was cooking something in the big iron pot. Geraldine watched his organised hands with a dreamy sensation that everything was somewhere else.

'Just pull your head in, that's all.' Was that Don?

'Ah, shut up.'

Geraldine smiled at Turner's back and had a vague thought that she must wash.

'My bloody spine's dislocated.' Bernard's sullen voice.

'You can say that again – every bump's a bone-shaker.'

'Every stone's a bum-shaker.' Noel's wit deteriorating.

'Just stop groaning and get stuck in, we're enjoying ourselves, remember?'

'Shit.'

Geraldine got some warm water from the fire in her plastic bowl.

'There she goes, bloody fussy old maid.'

'How about filling it up again, lady?'

'I'll do it,' a quiet voice said. Was it Turner?

In her tent Geraldine went through the ritual, starting at the top and working down. Their voices came from a great distance, angry, tired, childish. Fire from the sinking sun lit the blue canvas. Peace spread out inside her. Just like the first time. And like then, the sooner the better. It was her dominant will had brought the caravan to exactly the same spot on the map. The same will would survive the crack-up and take her back again, or rather onwards, this time free of the illusion of Noel. His worthlessness proved and removed.

The light was changing, paling, the sun gone down. The sulky quiet of anger exhausted hung about the campfire. Only Turner was unaffected, watching over his pot and stirring it now and then. Of the others two were washing themselves, another whittling a stick into a spear, two supine near the fire. They seemed already to understand she'd gone beyond them, that she was organised for freedom while they slumped in failure.

Jim stood at a short distance, still and silent. The sneaky dead circles were gone, and Geraldine knew that his blue eyes on her were waiting some opportunity. The disquiet she felt was momentary.

Turner called his mess chilli con carne. The joke fell flat. Each intent on anger, all with black looks, confirming that the expedition was ended. This the last night. In the morning there'd be the packing, the snarls, the departure. Only Turner didn't fit, calm and good-tempered. She got up.

Turner got up too. Geraldine moved towards her tent and found him beside her.

'Turning in early?' he said. He poked the tobacco in his pipe and got his matches out. Beyond him Geraldine saw the others sagging round the fire. 'Feeling a bit tricked? It shows in your face.'

She wanted to smile in disdain, but somehow the smile wouldn't come.

'Jim Oates, Nerida Jessop, your husband.' His voice was low and its gentleness a threat.

'I don't know what you're talking about.'

'You do.'

Geraldine turned to the tent, but his hand on her arm restrained her. She wrenched herself free. 'Don't touch me,' she hissed.

'Like to tell me about it?'

She stared at him. Who was this man Turner? So calm. She felt at bay and hated the feeling. What was he after? Poking his nose in on the basis of Jim's lying guesses. Now close up she could see his tired wrinkles, the careworn look in the big face. The breakdown would encompass Turner too, because even his armour showed signs of the little things that nibble away. Was he a friend of Jim's, a relative, perhaps? Whatever he was, what could he do? What was he saying?

' – and after his death in the crash your housekeeper revealed a great deal more than she realised. Your obsessive jealousy, for instance, that worried her. Then your swimming, and the switch from dislike to friendliness in your attitude to Miss Jessop. You told Mrs McIntyre the girl would never be a swimmer, and she couldn't understand why you were so pleased but put it down as just another one of your oddities. Then there were the preparations to go away with your husband and another sudden switch, overnight. Mrs McIntyre thought it peculiar the way you took both deaths so calmly, but out of loyalty she thought it must be shock.'

Geraldine listened in a dream.

'It fitted with the story you told my colleagues. All a bit too pat, Mrs Blaine.'

Turner was Thingummy, the one who'd left her with Somebody and Wells (water) while he went off setting sly traps for poor Mrs Mac. She'd thought from the start a detective, somewhere back near Cairns, pale and smudgy in newsprint.

'Then the curious entries in your diary.' At the look on her face he added, 'I took it from your handbag on the beach after you tried to drown Mr Oates.'

On impulse Geraldine struck out, but Turner caught both her arms. His pipe fell to the ground. There were staring faces round the fire.

'You'd better go to bed. Have you got a sleeping-pill?'

She nodded automatically.

'Then take a couple.'

This time he made no attempt to stop her when she turned. As she went in the tent Turner said, 'It's getting you down.'

Geraldine looked back at him. He had the smile she'd once thought nice, and the virile thighs and the masculinity and puffing pipe and the touch that of course was after all unbearable. She closed the flap, hating the watching stars.

His voice came through the canvas. 'You can't go on living with it, you're close to cracking, make sure you take the pills.'

Geraldine stood in the tent. Outside she could hear the

slithery whispers of death. A dreadful rigidity kept her motionless, and in her head someone was saying, 'Jim Oates, Nerida Jessop, your husband, Jim Oates, Nerida Jessop, your husband,' over and over, over and over.

Then she was in bed on the hateful stretcher. A silly name: Nerida Jessop. As silly as Lemming. And it was all over, all done, all past, darling Noel gone. Darling Noel. Her mind swept back to their first insatiable love. Six times a day before and after meals, not counting nights. Happy ever after. Her face wet with the tears so long crushed back. Darling Noel. The close hateful blue suffocating. No sleeping-pills.

Geraldine woke with a deep sense of outrage. A tremendous anger gripped her so that she was unable to think, or even to comprehend where she was. Why was she in a little tent? It was crazy, she loathed tents, someone had tricked her.

In a few moments she was dressed in shorts and shirt, the superior ritual of cleanliness forgotten. Her watch said five forty-five. She went outside. It was chilly and there were other tents. It came back to her then that this was the day of returning. Yet something was raging inside her. She left the campsite and started through the bush. Things scratched at her. Something to beat them with, then she could reach the thing quicker. She went back, ran lightly across the camp site, careful of spies watching, to the Land-Rover she shared with Jim. She scrabbled in the back for the long jack.

In the bush again she beat it aside and found the going easier. The panicky feeling was gone. Just a deep controlled rage leading her on to isolate and destroy the thing that must be annihilated for her own salvation and safety. The bush opened, soft short grass and a few trees. She was so silent, had to be, had to watch in silence until her chance came.

Then she saw it: grey, evil-eyed, motionless in its armour. Sharing her patch. Sharing the small haven which was all she had. Pretending innocence, wary, pretending it wasn't there. Each of them motionless. It began to trust her. The thing she hated trusted her. Eyes triangles of malice. Kill it and be rid of the misery, kill the thing destroying her life, the silly moronic smile in the grey scales, detested Nerida. Without a sound she raised the jack by slow millimetres. Then go back, to Noel and peace and the point of it all. Viciously she swung the jack and caught the thing's back.

'Careful now, Mrs Blaine.'

Geraldine turned her head and saw Turner, so very silly in his long khaki shorts. Such a pathetic man after all. Just a man with a job to do, and if this were his job it was up to him to do the best he could. She felt sorry for him as for all mediocrities. Because he didn't have a hope she'd play along with his stupidity. It might be amusing. But first finish off the thing she hated. The messy thing would soon be dead and would have been quite if Turner hadn't interrupted. Her strong hand tightened again on the jack but even before she could raise it there was a shot and the thing jerked and lay still. Her just vengeance usurped. Geraldine stared at Turner with his rifle. A brutal man, incurably stupid, and Jim there with him suddenly, from nowhere, with hate in his eyes looking at her. Jim should go with Nerida.

How desolate this place was, everything dead: bracken, leaves, branches, mangroves, the pale sea, the earth itself, all the dead stuff. Everywhere. What was Turner saying?

'Come along, Mrs Blaine, quietly now, no rough stuff.' His unrifled arm outstretched towards her.

Then Jim leaping between, lunging at her.

'Don't touch me,' Geraldine screamed.

But Turner had Jim and was soothing him in his quiet voice. 'She's mine, we agreed in Sydney, remember.'

'Killing a goanna!' Jim's voice was full of some enormity.

'It wasn't a goanna she was killing,' Turner the know-all said.

Then Turner's hand close and ready, but he didn't touch, looked startled at her face. Silly man, run-of-the-mill. Geraldine went with him, quiet and dignified. The world was so full of ordinariness. The point was somewhere ahead, beyond her vision. Just now her head was deliciously woolly.

———

CHAPTER 26

Turner's extra tent had been for her, he said, just in case. There was no need for it now. They flew by Royal Mail from Iron Range to Cairns, then got a plane to Sydney.

On the way Geraldine wept, but no one would see the tears behind her stony face. There was nobody she could tell how much she loved Noel. Nobody to understand. Nonentities. This man Turner, such a stupid man.

How could I harm Noel loving him so?

Turner said, 'Won't be long now. You all right?'

Such a silly man.

THE END

———

Patricia Mary Bryson Flower was born in Kent in 1928 and came to Australia at the age of fourteen, 'during her sonnet period'. She wrote 'off and on' from the age of eight, when she began her first book but never finished it. She also admits to having 'played left back in the school hockey team and moaned away among the contraltos of the school choir'. She married the artist, Cedric Flower, and capitalised on the associations of her new name in her lighter early novels, which have titles such as *Wax Flowers for Gloria* (1958) – jacket design by Cedric Flower – *Goodbye, Sweet William* (1959), *A Wreath of Water-Lilies* (1960), *One Rose Less* (1961) and *Hell for Heather* (1962). Four of these were published in Australia by Ure Smith, but most of her books were in The Crime Club series published by Collins in London and later ones were published in New York by Stein and Day as part of their Jubilee Mystery series. Most of her novels seem to have been translated into French, German (Wilhelm Goldmann's Krimi series in the early 1970s) and Italian. She also wrote many radio and television plays and some satirical sketches for Sydney's New Theatre, winning the Mary Gilmore Award for a one-hour TV play in 1967. Her television play, The Tape Recorder, was the BBC's first drama to be transmitted in colour. In 1978 she committed suicide, gassing herself.

She once wrote: 'People sometimes ask as they edge away, Why murder? I'm absorbed in character, not in murder. In ordinary people a bit round the bend. I like to follow the effects on my characters of heredity, environment and circumstance, and reveal in action, reaction and interaction the instability which might in real life go unnoticed but in my books is fatal. For my crackpots, murder is the only way out. Instead of moving to another town, or trying sweet reason, they resort to the "final solution". And find, of course, that it isn't.

'My murders are climatic as well as climactic. I fancy that certain climates breed types of murder (eg England – dank wallpaper and floorboards) and that even something as fleeting as a weather change may turn the screw. Impulse and trivia, too. A domestic flare-up. Marriage is a fine breeding-ground.

'Why murder? seems an irrelevant question in the world today. It's a relief to turn from mass murder and mayhem to a private controllable murder of my own; to manipulate characters in chessboard conditions. It's the real world that is unpredictable and far, far crazier.'

Pat Flower's later crime novels, those on which her considerable critical reputation rests (though they are not very well known in Australia), are quite different in tone from the early ones, which may be classed with those of Jennifer Rowe. The late ones belong to that group of psychological thrillers associated with such powerful writers as Patricia Highsmith and Ruth Rendell (Barbara Vine). Nevertheless, the first of the 'floral' novels, *Wax Flowers for Gloria*, presents a character who is recognizably similar in type to the anti-heroine of *Vanishing Point*: 'Gloria had the strength of application, she kept her goal in view through petty frustrations of every day. Her ambition was limited, her optimism easy. Nothing came into her view of the world that had no bearing upon herself. She was the centre of the universe and the universe was small.'

Vanishing Point is a serious novel with a sociopathic murderer held unwaveringly in its focus. It is a work of art as a painting or a photograph is and its style is perhaps best regarded as a series of snapshots. At the centre of the picture,

Geraldine Blaine struggles to achieve a certain clarity; at the periphery are bright colours, noises and more or less blurred human figures, flickering in and out of the range of Geraldine's carefully filtered attention. For, although she pretends to be in search of a precise vision, Geraldine cannot bear very much reality and is happiest when cocooned in a kind of fuzzy blur, the state in which she finally settles: 'The point was somewhere ahead, beyond her vision. Just now her head was deliciously woolly.' Technically, a vanishing point is a term of perspective, the point in which receding parallel lines, if continued, appear to meet.

Geraldine, who is presented in 'sympathetic' third person, has a tone of voice which may remind us at times of Penelope Keith in *The Good Life*, trying unavailingly to maintain high social and aesthetic values in a dirty, vulgar world, or, more sinister, of Diana Rigg in *Mother Love*, asserting rigid standards of loyalty to the point of smothering whomever she chooses to love. That both of these figures from television find an Australian echo in Dame Edna Everage is not surprising; Geraldine trembles on the brink of hysterical black farce just as Edna hovers on the point of launching into a murderous assault.

The unprepared reader of *Vanishing Point* may find the book's structure bewildering at first: after suffering all the gruelling tedium and discomfort of the sweaty, foul-tempered and abortive journey into Far North Queensland, it is a lot to ask that we should go through it a second time, following those dazzling explosive shocks of violence in the second part. But this is a book to admire in retrospect rather than to enjoy. Oddly, it is more enjoyable the second time around. What at first was excruciating (because a first reader always wants to be rushed to the 'point' of a thriller) becomes fascinating. The second safari, on a second reading particularly, has the sort of pleasure one associates with a classical Greek tragedy: the setting is familiar (though by no means quite the same as that we have known from before), but the inner pressure, the inexorable workings of fate assisted by the human agents Jim and the principal stage manager, Turner, are far more powerful than we expected. Turner is so named, I suppose because he turns the screw.

Pat Flower employs a great economy of means, a restricted palette. If we consider the peripheral figures, we find they are characterised often as mere 'voices' or colours. They are set at a distance, beyond focal length. It happened that Pat Flower was herself an 'optically challenged' person. An early biographical note explains: 'Her eyesight is poor and her vision often awry, but her mind is fairly orderly. She prefers reading plays to seeing them as, owing to her poor sight, what she sees is frequently at variance with the text – she often falls out with her husband over visits to the theatre.'

No doubt this handicap was converted to a strength by the novelist, much as Renoir or El Greco exploited the distinctive subjective qualities of their own impressions of 'actual' life. Geraldine wilfully refuses to learn the surnames or even the sex of most of those among whom she is thrust, though she becomes obsessively interested in the elect few, seeing these, however, astigmatically, the way she chooses to see them, and expecting them to conform to her vision. When she learns the christian name of Turner, she giggles and rejects it: Turner is just Turner. She wishes to choose the significant (epithetical) names of people: it is 'darling Noel', 'dear Mrs Mac', 'vulgar drunken Clyde', 'poor Jim', 'detested Nerida'. She speaks of herself in similar terms: 'Geraldine Whatsaname (rejecting even his name)'. Sometimes the style even seems to mimic the banality of the Janet and John books, reflecting satirically, perhaps, Geraldine's mental age. By the same token, the comments we hear about Geraldine are usually just as crudely dismissive or impercipient – 'zombie', 'raving ratbag' (if that really is meant for her).

The third person narrative allows us to see Geraldine proceeding through her year of misery as if she were acting a part to an unresponsive or despicable audience. At first the point of the exercise is to impress upon Noel how much she loves him: this is why she goes (and keeps going) on the bush trek after he has abandoned both it and her. His vanishing proves a point that Geraldine refuses to accept. Occasionally, nevertheless, she experiences moments of truth, of seeing the point. When at the end of chapter eleven Geraldine recognises the crucial difference between Nerida and herself, the mask of her persona drops and the naked 'I' is exposed:

'Geraldine was in bed when Noel came up. She'd looked at herself in the glass and thought of Nerida, of Nerida's skin, of Noel kissing that skin goodnight, all over.

'I was never like that, glowing like that.

'It wasn't make-up. Nerida's shine came from inside, from something transcending youth.

'Even at nineteen I was never like that.'

It is a moment of despair and Geraldine turns her face to the wall.

Geraldine rarely refers to her early life: this is not the sort of novel in which the narrator confesses the sins committed against her as she reclines comfortably upon the psychiatrist's couch, all passion spent. We hear enough all the same, even from such a small detail as her detestation of the colour pink, first mentioned in chapter two, which goes back to her mother's discovery of her father, Gerald Smith, *in flagrante delicto* with a 'tall thin woman in pink who rode a motor-scooter'. Geraldine was then eleven. This experience from early childhood helps to account for her pathological aversion to the al fresco breakfast in chapter twenty-two, when Jim is seen with 'pink slime from the tinned spaghetti all over his face'. Geraldine's reaction is to clean up the whole camp, an unprecedented exertion for her, not only dumping 'the pale pink slimy worms of uneaten spaghetti' and the other rubbish and burying it, but burying the remaining cans of the stuff, as well, just to enforce the point. Her mother had thought Gerald (aged forty-three) a 'dirty old man', but Geraldine, left with a longing for a father-husband who is as he should be, clean and strong, edits this into 'a girl in a dirty shirt of hateful pink'.

Because she is supersensitive to slights, to the eyes upon her, and pathologically averse to being touched (except by her one current special person), Geraldine prefers to live in a world shut off or withdrawn from that in which the others live. To call her world a cocoon is peculiarly apt, because she sees herself as one always about to emerge. On the rare occasions when she does break out of the shell, when she is the one who does the touching or the speaking, she can be magnificently devastating. One thinks of the savage dramatic irony in the scene in chapter twenty-four, where the characters of Jim and Turner are coming into sharp resolution for the reader but are not yet clear to Geraldine:

'Turner's voice came. "She'd feel justified, you know, the wife. Feel she was right, exacting justice. We had a schizo bloke did much the same a couple of years ago."

'"I'll be glad when she gets what's coming," Jim said in a savage voice.

'Geraldine felt a surge of compassion for Jim. Not because of his girl but because he let it eat him up. He couldn't unbend. You'd think up here, a continent away – it was puzzling that anyone could so give in to self-pity. She edged towards him. "I'm terribly sorry about your girl," she said in a sweet voice.

'Jim flinched as though he'd been stung.'

What Geraldine actually felt when she murdered Nerida is much more deeply ambiguous than the grave Turner, 'such a silly man', could suppose. It is an act not of justice, not even of exorcism; it is very hard to say just what it is. Perhaps it is best explained as an act of self-cleansing lust, a kind of cathartic rape. Flower's account of the drowning of Nerida may be one of the most brilliant passages of writing about intimate violence in our literature.

The title of *Vanishing Point* is obviously a whole complex of puns. From the beginning, puns are associated with Noel:

'Cape York Puninsula, he called it. Now and again he said with his smile, "Where's the point?" and squeezed Geraldine's arm or touched her breast. Dear silly Noel. Last night in the dying fire she thought he'd touched Julie. She hated Noel to touch anyone else.'

Cape York Peninsula is an obvious metaphor for the vanishing point of perspective, shaped as it is on the map like a huge mountain reaching from the continental mass up beyond Cairns towards Papua New Guinea. Even today the road to the 'top end' is not to be undertaken lightly, but Flower makes it seem an ordeal to rank with Marlow's expedition up the Congo in *Heart of Darkness*, though for Geraldine the danger is always from the weakness within her rather than from any hostile cruelty endemic in the environment.

Geraldine divides the journey northwards itself into points: Brisbane is 'a point they must pass before she could guide Noel back' (into her ideal of their relationship); there are so many rivers to cross. The camps set up along the way are like those in an assault on Everest, an analogy not used directly by Flower but reminiscent of the pointlessness of the whole proceeding: 'A pointless journey that Geraldine must give point to.' Everest is to be climbed because it is there; Cape York is to be reached (or not), first because Noel is there, then because he is not: he has vanished and missed the point. Noel's puns have point but lack subtlety: he knows that a nipple is a point, that a penis is a point. Noel would not see it, but Flower knows and Geraldine perhaps intuits that the inner shape of Nerida's thighs establish another Cape York Peninsula, vanishing towards an un-nameable 'hated junction' that must be gripped in a kind of practical zeugma. Tragically for Geraldine, the yoke of marriage could not provide the promised opposite to what Nerida, Julie and the others represent, the 'mutual passion, a shared ecstasy, the emptiness ended', since Noel is now 'so remote it was a stranger sharing her bedroom. Physically wasn't enough, she wanted all of Noel. Marriage was only a small part, perhaps had fouled things up, because Noel began receding at once, even during their honeymoon. She couldn't grasp hold of him. When she wanted the strength of a rock, or a great mountain, he was elusive, the water that ran off the mountain. Even when they strained together – perhaps then most of all. He ran through her fingers, dodged the bind of her loving female web. She was left with nothing and no way to fill it up, no pretence that the nothing wasn't there'.

It is easy to think of Geraldine as a female spider, who does not even wish to share her husband with their children and so makes him, as he keeps on telling her with his dreadful puns, lose his point by a vasectomy. Killing Noel is only reifying his nothingness, confirming the point of his evanishment.

After her success in establishing her own reality, Noel's irreality and the worthlessness of the whole world outside, it would be conventional for Geraldine to retreat into suicide. Instead she chooses to continue searching for the point that has eluded her by the weakness of Noel and the others. Hence comes her interest in Jim – and her reaction once she discovers his hostility, another betrayer. Hence comes her infatuation with Turner – and her refusal to accept his superior strength and will. At the end there is no longer any point; she must vanish into herself. The silly vulgar people outside have a sneering joke about that kind of action, but we will refrain from making it.

MICHAEL J. TOLLEY AND PETER MOSS

WAKEFIELD CRIME CLASSICS

Peter Moss and Michael J. Tolley, general editors of the Wakefield Crime Classics series, are colleagues at the University of Adelaide. Late in 1988, they began assembling a series of Australian 'classic' crime fiction and soon realised that the problem was not going to be one of finding sufficient works of high quality, but of finding a bold enough publisher fired with the same vision.

This series revives forgotten or neglected gems of crime and mystery fiction by Australian authors. Many of the writers have established international reputations but are little known in Australia. In the wake of the excitement generated by the new wave of Australian crime fiction writers, we hope that the achievements of earlier days can be justly celebrated.

If you wish to be informed about new books as they are released in the Wakefield Crime Classics series, send your name and address to Wakefield Press, Box 2266, Kent Town, South Australia 5071, phone (08) 362 8800, fax (08) 362 7592.